The Crossing
Adrian Cox

Chapter 1

The sun breaks over the horizon like a promise, flooding the Great Eastern Highway in gold. I stand at the roadside with my thumb out, my small brown leather suitcase at my feet, and I can't stop smiling. The air smells different out here, cleaner somehow, emptier. Free.

I smooth down my red polka dot shift dress, the white dots catching the early light. My white go-go boots are already dusty from the shoulder of the road, but I don't care. I feel cute. I feel alive. For the first time in forever, I feel like I'm exactly where I'm supposed to be.

A few cars have passed already. One slowed down, an older man with grey whiskers peering at me through his windscreen, but something about his eyes made my stomach twist, so I looked away. He drove on. Good. I don't need just any ride. I need the right one.

Then I see it, a Volvo 144GL, cream coloured, coming up the highway. It passes me, and for a moment my heart sinks, but then brake lights flare red. The car pulls onto the shoulder about fifty yards ahead.

I just know this is the one. I grab my suitcase and run.

By the time I reach the passenger door, I'm breathless and grinning. I yank it open and there he is, a man in his thirties with long hair, a thin mustard-coloured turtleneck sweater, brown bell-bottomed trousers, and aviator sunglasses pushed up on his head. He's smiling at me, warm and genuine.

"Hey there!" he says. "Do you need a lift? It's not safe for a young lady to be out on the road alone. Where are you headed?"

"I want to get as far away from Perth as I can," I say, the words tumbling out before I can stop them.

His smile widens. "Well, hop in baby, I'm driving all the way to Adelaide."

Adelaide. The word sounds like music. I put my suitcase in the footwell and climb into the passenger seat, pulling the door shut. The interior smells like old vinyl and coffee and something else, something masculine and safe.

"Would you like to put the seatbelt on?" he asks, reaching toward me.

I glance down at the strange strap hanging beside my shoulder. "Erm?"

"Oh, you've not worn one before, here," he says, and suddenly he's leaning across me. My breathing quickens. His arm brushes against mine as he pulls the belt across my body. I hear the click as it locks into place, and then the belt tightens against my chest, pinning me back against the seat.

"No, no, no," I whisper, my hands flying to the strap. My vision starts to tunnel.

"Hey, hey, don't worry baby, it's all groovy," he says quickly, reaching over to unclip it. The belt whips back with a snap, and I can breathe again. "Not everyone has used a seatbelt before. They can feel restrictive. By the way, I'm David."

David. I look at him properly now, really look at him. His face is kind. Open. There's something about his eyes that makes me feel... known.

"Mary," I manage to say.

"Nice to meet you, Mary." He smiles again, this time with a little chuckle, pulls his aviators down over his eyes, and we merge back onto the highway.

For a long while, I just watch the landscape roll past. The city falls away behind us, and soon there's nothing but red earth and scrubby bush and endless sky. It's the most beautiful thing I've ever seen. I can't remember the last time I saw this much space, this much nothing.

A billboard appears on the side of the road, advertisement for Palmolive soap. A man in a suit, smiling, holding up a bar of soap. But it's his eyes. Those eyes. They're looking right at me. Following me as we pass.

I turn away quickly, facing forward, my chest heaving. The eyes. Always the eyes.

One, two, three. One, two, three. One, two, three.

"You okay?" David asks.

I force myself to nod. "Yes. Fine."

But my hands are gripping the edge of the seat. One, two, three. One, two, three.

A bird, I think it's a kite, soars high above the road, riding the thermals in wide, lazy circles. I watch it until my neck aches, until it's just a dark speck against the blue. That's what I want to be. Just like that.

David keeps glancing over at me. I catch him doing it, looking across with that same warm smile, like he's checking I'm still there, still okay. It's not creepy or strange. It's... protective somehow. Sympathetic. Like he understands something about me without me having to say it.

"The scenery out here is amazing, isn't it?" he says after a while.

"Yes," I breathe. "It's beautiful. So much space."

I wind down the window and stick my arm out, stretching it as far as it will go. The wind rushes past my fingers, and I imagine I'm flying, soaring up above the road, above the car, above everything. I close my eyes and let the wind whip through my hair. Up here, I'm a bird. Light. Weightless. Free.

After a while, I pull my arm back in, still smiling, the wind having worked some kind of magic on me. When I glance at David, he's smiling too. That same gentle smile.

"You look happy," he says.

"I am," I tell him, and it's the truest thing I've said in... I don't know how long.

"That's groovy baby." He glances at me again. "You must like music then. Who's your artist? I used to be into the Beach Boys, but now I'm more into the Stones, man."

"Oh, anything," I say, though I'm not entirely sure that's true. "I don't have a favourite. My mother used to sing me songs when I was little. I liked *them*."

The memory surfaces unexpected and soft, my mother's voice, gentle and clear, singing me to sleep. I can almost hear it now, beneath the rush of wind through the window.

"Groovy," David says warmly. He reaches for the radio dial. "Want to hear what's on?"

"No..." I start to say, but he's already turning it on.

The crackling erupts through the speakers, loud and violent, and then voices start booming out as he tunes through stations. Static and talking and music and static and voices voices voices.

"No, no, no!" I'm hitting the radio, slapping at the dial, at the buttons, anywhere to make it stop.

David quickly switches it off. The silence is like a physical thing.

"Are you okay?" he asks, concern thick in his voice.

I'm breathing hard. My hands are shaking. "Yes. Sorry. I don't like the radio. It's on all the time at home. At Greenplace. I just can't take all the voices anymore."

"It's okay baby, we can travel without it," he says gently. He doesn't ask questions. Doesn't push. Just accepts it.

I look out the window again, trying to calm my racing heart. The land stretches on forever, empty and open. Mine.

I put my arm back out the window, fully stretched. Close my eyes. Pretend I'm flying. The wind rushes past and I imagine I'm up in the clouds, far above everything, far from home and the radio and everything that came before.

Up here, there are no walls. No schedules. No one telling me when to wake, when to eat, when to sleep. No locked doors.

Just sky.

Just freedom.

Just me and the wind and David's car carrying me toward something new.

When I open my eyes again, I realise I'm smiling.

For the first time in longer than I can remember, I'm actually, genuinely happy.

Chapter 2

David woke with a start, his hand reaching across the bed before his eyes were fully open.

Empty.

The sheets were cold. He bolted upright, heart hammering. "Mary?"

The motel room was small enough to see everything at once, the bathroom door stood open, dark. Her suitcase was gone from the chair where she'd left it. His own bag sat by the door, untouched.

"Shit. Shit, shit, shit."

He scrambled out of bed, yanking on his trousers, not bothering with his shoes. The digital clock on the bedside table read 6:47 AM. How long had she been gone? He'd fallen asleep around midnight, maybe later. She'd been right there beside him, her breathing soft and even. He remembered stroking her hair, thinking how peaceful she looked.

He threw open the door. The parking lot was nearly empty, just his Volvo and a rusted-out ute three spaces down. The highway stretched out in both directions, grey and endless in the early morning light.

"Mary!" His voice cracked.

Nothing. Just the distant call of crows and the hum of the highway.

David ran back inside, grabbed his keys and wallet, shoved his feet into his shoes without tying them. His mind raced through possibilities. Had she wandered off? Had she had another episode?

No. No, she'd taken her suitcase. She'd left on purpose.

He got in the car, started the engine, and pulled onto the highway heading east. She'd want to keep going, wouldn't she? Toward Adelaide. Toward the future. Unless...

Unless she didn't remember any of it.

His hands gripped the steering wheel hard enough to hurt. He should have been more careful. Should have watched for the signs. But last night she'd seemed so present, so there. They'd had dinner at the motel diner, nothing fancy, just burgers and chips, and she'd smiled at him the whole time. Really smiled. They'd talked about Adelaide, about the apartment he'd lined up, about starting fresh. She'd held his hand.

And then they'd come back to the room, and everything had seemed fine.

The sun was climbing now, turning the sky from grey to pink to gold. David scanned the roadside, looking for any sign of her. A flash of red. White boots. Anything.

There, about two miles out from the motel, a figure on the shoulder of the road. Thumb out. Red dress.

Relief flooded through him so intensely he nearly veered off the road. He slowed down, getting closer. Yes. Yes, it was her. Mary, standing there like she was waiting for any stranger to come along.

He drove past her, he had to, couldn't just slam on the brakes, and pulled over about fifty yards ahead. In his rear-view mirror, he watched her grab her suitcase and start running toward him.

David's heart was still hammering, but now it was mixed with something else. Dread. Because he knew, even before she opened the door, even before he saw that bright, hopeful smile on her face, that she didn't remember. Didn't remember last night. Didn't remember him.

The passenger door opened and there she was, breathless and grinning, her eyes full of excitement and trust and not a single trace of recognition.

"Hey there!" He kept his voice steady, warm, even though panic clawed at his chest. "Do you need a lift? It's not safe for a young lady to be out on the road alone. Where are you headed?"

"I want to get as far away from Perth as I can," she said.

Perth. She thought she was still in Perth. They were in Norseman, nearly four hundred kilometres away.

"Well, hop in baby, I'm driving all the way to Adelaide," he said.

She climbed in, putting her suitcase in the footwell, and David felt the weight of it settle in his chest. This was bad. This was really bad. But what could he do? Tell her the truth? That they'd spent last night together.

She'd panic. She'd run. Or worse, she'd look at him with that vacant, terrified expression he'd seen before.

So, he played along. Went through the motions. Showed her the seatbelt, he should have remembered she hated restraints, should have known better, and watched her panic. Watched her calm down. Introduced himself like they were strangers.

She told him her name was Mary, and he pretended he didn't already know.

As they drove, David kept glancing over at her. She was looking out the window with this expression of wonder, like she'd never seen open sky before. Which, in a way, maybe she hadn't. Not for a long time.

He'd wanted to give her that. Just this chance. Just to show her there was a world waiting, a life they could build together. He'd been so careful planning it, mapped out the route, booked the motel rooms, even had the apartment in Adelaide already sorted. He'd been saving for years, ever since that night in 1969 when he'd watched Neil Armstrong step onto the moon.

That broadcast had changed everything for David. He'd been twenty-five, sitting in the park with his mates, high as a kite, passing around a joint and talking shit about nothing. Someone had brought a portable TV, powered by a car battery, and they'd all gathered around to watch. Most of his friends had laughed it off, called it government propaganda, gone back to their drugs and their philosophy about dropping out and living free.

But David had stared at that grainy black-and-white image of a man walking on the moon, and something had cracked open inside him. While everyone else saw a hoax or a waste of money, he saw possibility. He saw what human beings could do when they actually tried, when they pushed past the easy comfort of drugs and rhetoric and aimed for something bigger.

The next morning, he'd flushed his stash down the toilet. Quit the park scene. Got a job at a warehouse, saved every penny he could. Enrolled in night classes at technical college. Studied engineering with a focus that would have seemed impossible to the man he'd been just months before.

It had taken six years. Six years of night classes and textbooks and going to bed exhausted every night. Six years of his old friends asking when he'd stop being so uptight, when he'd come back and hang loose with them again. Six years of proving to himself that he was capable of more than he'd ever imagined.

And then, last year, he'd gotten the letter. The Australian Space Agency wanted him. Wanted him. David Morrison, former dropout and stoner, was going to help build the future.

The job didn't start until January, but he'd already lined up the apartment in Adelaide. Already imagined his new life there, clean and purposeful and aimed at the stars.

And then he'd met Mary.

He watched her stick her arm out the window now, eyes closed, pretending to fly. The wind whipped her hair around her face and she was smiling, really smiling.

When he'd first met her, she'd been so fragile, so broken. It had taken months before she'd even look at him properly. Months more before she'd smiled. But gradually, carefully, she'd let him in. Let him see the person underneath all that pain and confusion.

He'd fallen for her. Completely. Stupidly. And he'd thought, maybe foolishly, that if he could just get her away, give her a fresh start, she could heal. They could build something together.

But now, watching her pretend she didn't know him, David wondered if he'd been lying to himself all along.

She pulled her arm back in and looked at him, and for just a second something flickered in her eyes.

"You look happy," he said.

"I am," she told him.

He tried to keep the conversation light after that. Talked about music. Let her tell him about her mother's singing, he'd heard the story before, but he listened like it was new. When he reached for the radio without thinking and she started panicking, hitting the dashboard, he shut it off immediately.

"It's okay baby, we can travel without it," he said, keeping his voice gentle.

They drove in silence for a while after that. David's mind was racing, trying to figure out what to do. Adelaide was still two days away. Two days of driving across the Nullarbor with Mary not remembering who he was, not remembering why they were together.

He reached into his pocket and pulled out a small tin of mints. Inside were eight white tablets, carefully wrapped in tissue. Her medication. He was supposed to give her one every morning, one every evening. Keep her stable. Keep the episodes at bay.

But if he offered them to her now, she'd ask questions. Want to know why he had them. Want to know why he thought she needed them.

"Hey," he said casually, "you want some candy? Picked these up at the motel. Peppermints."

He held out the tin, hoping she wouldn't look too closely, hoping she'd just take one and swallow it without thinking.

Mary glanced at the tin, then at him, and for a long moment she just stared. David's heart hammered. Did she know? Did she remember?

Then she smiled. "Sure. Thank you."

She took one of the tablets, popped it in her mouth, and swallowed it dry.

David let out a breath he didn't know he'd been holding. "Good. That's good."

He put the tin back in his pocket and kept driving, watching the road stretch out ahead of them, red and empty and impossibly long.

Somewhere out there was Adelaide. Somewhere out there was the life he'd imagined, the fresh start they both needed.

But first, they had to cross the Nullarbor. Had to get through whatever was coming.

And David couldn't shake the feeling that the hardest part was still ahead of them.

Chapter 3

A kangaroo appears suddenly from behind a clump of saltbush, bounding across the scrubland in great leaps. I press my face to the window, watching it go, so fast, so graceful, each jump carrying it further and further away. I wish I could move like that. Just bound away when... when what?

The thought slips away before I can catch it, leaving only a hollow feeling in my chest.

"We'll need to stop for petrol soon," David says, breaking the comfortable silence we've settled into. "And probably get something to eat. You hungry?"

I realise I am. "Yes. I think so."

"There's a roadhouse about thirty kilometres ahead. Should have food."

Thirty kilometres.

The numbers feel strange in my mouth when I try to picture them. How far is that? How long? Time and distance have become slippery things out here, where there are no landmarks, no boundaries, nothing to measure against.

We drive in silence for a while longer. I keep my arm out the window, letting the wind rush through my fingers.

The sun is high now, hot on my face. I close my eyes and just feel it, the heat, the wind, the movement of the car carrying me forward.

When I open them again, David is looking at me with that same soft smile.

"You really do love that, don't you?" he says.

"What?"

"The wind. The flying feeling."

I nod. "It's like... I don't know. Like I'm not stuck anymore."

Something crosses his face, sadness, maybe, or understanding, but he just nods and turns his attention back to the road.

I stare out at the landscape. Red earth. Scrubby bushes. Empty sky. It all looks exactly the same as it did an hour ago.

Exactly the same.

My chest tightens.

"We're going in circles."

"What?" David glances at me.

"We're going in circles. Or, or you've turned around. You're taking me back." My voice is rising. "Everything looks the same. We haven't moved. We're not going anywhere."

"Mary, no, we're still heading east. I promise. It just... the Nullarbor all looks similar. That's why they call it the longest straight road in Australia. It's supposed to look the same for a while."

"No." I shake my head, panic clawing up my throat. "No, I've seen that exact bush before. That exact rock. We've been here. You're lying to me. You're taking me back to..."

"Mary, look at me." David's voice is gentle but firm. "I'm not taking you back. I'm not lying to you. We're going to Adelaide, just like I said. The landscape just looks repetitive out here, but we're making progress. I promise."

I want to believe him. But everything does look the same. How can I know we're actually moving forward? How can I know he's not just driving me around and around until...

"There," David says, pointing ahead. "See?"

The roadhouse appears like a mirage on the horizon. A low concrete building with a tin roof, two petrol pumps out front, and a faded sign that reads "NULLARBOR ROADHOUSE - FUEL - FOOD - REPAIRS." A handful of cars and trucks are scattered in the dirt parking area.

Something new. Something different. We really are moving forward.

The panic in my chest loosens slightly. I take a breath. "Okay. Okay."

David reaches over and squeezes my hand briefly. "See? We're getting there. I promise."

David pulls up to one of the pumps and cuts the engine. "I'll fill her up. You want to go inside, use the bathroom, stretch your legs?"

"Okay."

I climb out of the car, my legs stiff from sitting. The heat hits me immediately, dry and intense, pressing down on my shoulders like a physical thing.

I smooth down my dress, suddenly aware of how dusty my white boots have become.

Inside, the roadhouse is dim and cool. A woman behind the counter, probably in her fifties, grey hair pulled back in a tight bun, looks up as I enter. Her eyes flick over me, pausing on my dress, my boots. She doesn't say anything, but I catch the slight raise of her eyebrows.

I look down at myself, then back at her. "It's his favourite dress," I say blankly.

The woman's expression softens slightly, misunderstanding. "That's sweet, love."

I turn and look out through the window at the car, at David filling the tank. But I'm not thinking about David.

"Bathroom?" I ask, turning back.

She points toward a door marked "LADIES" at the back.

As I walk past the counter, I notice a newspaper lying there. The masthead reads "The West Australian" and below it, in smaller print: "Friday, November 18, 1977."

1977.

The numbers don't make sense. I stare at them, trying to make them fit into place, but they keep sliding away from me like water through my fingers. David said it was 1977. The newspaper says 1977. But that can't be right. It was just 1967. Wasn't it? Or was it '68? When did Mother...

My head starts to hurt.

"You alright, love?" the woman asks.

I look up. She's watching me with a mixture of concern and suspicion.

"Yes. Fine. Just... the bathroom."

I hurry past her and lock myself in the small, dingy bathroom. Splash cold water on my face. Look at myself in the spotted mirror. Same red dress. Same white boots. Same face, somehow, older. But something feels wrong, like I'm wearing someone else's clothes, living in someone else's life.

Ten years. Ten years missing. Where did they go?

A knock on the door makes me jump.

"Mary? You okay in there?"

David's voice. Gentle. Worried.

"Yes. I'm coming."

I dry my face and open the door. He's standing there with two paper-wrapped sandwiches and two bottles of Coke.

"Got us some lunch," he says.

We sit at one of the plastic tables near the window. The sandwich is white bread and limp lettuce and some kind of processed meat, but I eat it anyway. David watches me between bites of his own sandwich.

"You seemed upset back there," he says carefully. "At the counter."

I take a sip of Coke, the sweetness almost too much. "The newspaper. The date."

He's quiet for a moment. Then: "What about it?"

"It said 1977. But that doesn't... I don't..." I trail off, not knowing how to explain the confusion, the missing pieces.

David reaches across the table and takes my hand. His palm is warm, calloused. "Hey. It's okay. Sometimes time gets... confusing. That's normal."

"Is it?"

"For some people, yeah." He squeezes my hand gently. "What's the last thing you remember clearly? Before today, I mean."

I try to think. There are fragments—Mother singing, the house by the river, my room with the window looking out at the sky. But they're all jumbled together, no clear order, no connecting thread.

"I don't know," I whisper. "I don't know."

"That's okay," David says again. His voice is so kind it makes my chest hurt. "You don't have to know. We're just driving to Adelaide, yeah? That's all that matters. Just you and me and the road."

I nod, wanting to believe him. Wanting this simple story to be true.

After lunch, we get back in the car. The afternoon stretches ahead of us, long and hot.

I'm settling into the seat, adjusting myself, when my hand brushes against something in the door pocket. I pull it out without thinking. A knife. Large. Heavy. The blade catches the sunlight streaming through the windscreen.

"Jesus Christ!" David jerks the wheel slightly, then steadies it. "Mary, where did you get that?"

I look at the knife in my hand. It feels familiar. Right. "It's for safety," I say. "Just in case."

"Just in case of what?" His voice is tight, controlled panic underneath. "Mary, did you buy that? Did you, did you steal it from the roadhouse?"

I try to remember. Did I buy it? Did I take it? The memories are slippery. All I know is that I need it. For safety.

"Just in case," I repeat, my voice flat.

"Mary, that's..." David runs his hand through his hair. "That's a weapon. You can't just carry around a weapon like that."

"It's for safety," I say again. Why doesn't he understand?

"From what? From who?" He's looking at me now, really looking, and there's something in his eyes I haven't seen before. Fear. Not of me, maybe, but of something. "Mary, are you planning to hurt someone? Are you planning to hurt yourself?"

"No." The word comes out too quick. "It's just in case. In case he..." I stop. In case who? The thought slips away.

David takes a breath. "Okay. Okay. How about this, we keep it for safety, like you said. But let's put it somewhere safe. Under my seat, yeah? That way we both know where it is, but it's not just... sitting out."

I consider this. The knife under his seat. Still there. Still available if I need it.

"For safety," I agree.

"For safety," David echoes. He holds out his hand.

I give him the knife. He reaches down and slides it under his seat, far back where it can't be seen. When he sits up again, I see him let out a breath he'd been holding.

"Okay," he says. "Okay."

We drive in silence after that. The easy warmth from before has cooled.

David keeps glancing at me like he's trying to figure something out. I turn to look out the window, watching the landscape blur past.

After maybe an hour, David pulls off onto the shoulder. "I need to take a leak," he says. "You okay here for a minute?"

I nod.

He gets out, walks a little way into the scrub. I watch him go, then turn back to face forward.

The road stretches out ahead. Empty. Endless. Adelaide is out there somewhere. Just keep going. Just keep moving forward.

I open the door and start walking.

One foot in front of the other. The red earth is warm under my boots. The sun is hot on my face. Adelaide. I'll get to Adelaide. I'll find help. David's car broke down, and he needs help and I have to get to Adelaide to.

A sound behind me. An engine.

I turn. David's car is moving, pulling up alongside me. The window rolls down.

"Mary! What are you doing?"

I smile at him, relieved. "You fixed it! The car, it was broken down and I was going to Adelaide to get help for you, but you fixed it!"

David's face does something complicated. "Mary, the car wasn't broken down. We just stopped so I could use the bathroom. You were in the car, and then..." He stops. "Get in. Please."

I climb in, still smiling. "I'm glad you fixed it. I was worried I wouldn't make it in time."

David doesn't say anything. He just puts the car in gear and starts driving again.

The silence is different now. Heavier. After a while, I glance over and see his jaw is tight, his hands gripping the wheel harder than they need to.

"Are you okay?" I ask.

He looks at me, and there's something in his eyes, doubt, maybe, or fear, or something else I can't quite name.

"Yeah," he says finally. "Yeah, I'm okay."

But I'm not sure either of us believes it.

We pass the occasional vehicle going the other direction, trucks mostly, and one caravan being pulled by a station wagon. Each time, David lifts his hand in a wave and the other driver waves back. It feels like a ritual, this acknowledgment between travellers crossing the emptiness together.

The sun is starting to lower toward the horizon when David speaks again.

"We're going to stop for the night soon," he says. "Not at a motel or anything. I thought we could camp out.

Under the stars. If that's okay with you?"

Camp out. Under the stars. The thought fills me with something like joy.

"Yes," I say. "I'd like that."

"Good." He smiles. "There's a spot I know, about another hour up the road. Nice and quiet. Middle of nowhere."

Middle of nowhere. Perfect.

As the sun sinks lower, painting the sky in shades of orange and pink and purple, David pulls off the highway onto a dirt track. We bounce along for a few minutes until the road disappears entirely and we're just driving across open scrubland. Finally, he stops and cuts the engine.

Silence. Complete and total silence. No cars. No voices. No radio. Just the ticking of the cooling engine and the distant call of a bird.

"Here we are," David says. "Our hotel for the night."

We get out. The air is cooler now, the heat of the day evaporating into the vast sky. David opens the boot and pulls out a blanket and a small cooler.

"I packed some supplies," he says. "Sandwiches, water, some fruit. And these."

He holds up the tin of peppermints. "Want one? They're good for settling your stomach after a long drive."

I take one and swallow it. It tastes slightly bitter, but I don't mind.

David spreads the blanket on the ground a little way from the car. We sit down, and I realize just how tired I am. My whole body aches from sitting all day, but it's a good ache. The ache of moving, of going somewhere.

The sky above us deepens from blue to purple to black, and then the stars begin to appear. First just a few, then dozens, then hundreds, then so many I can't even begin to count them. I've never seen so many stars. At Greenplace, the lights are always on, and even when they're not, there are never this many stars visible.

"Beautiful, isn't it?" David says softly.

I can't speak. I just nod.

He lies back on the blanket, and after a moment, I do too. We lie there side by side, staring up at the infinite sky.

"You see that bright one there?" David points. "That's Venus. And that cluster? That's the Pleiades. Seven sisters, they're called in Greek mythology."

"Tell me about them," I say.

So, he does. He tells me about the seven sisters who were turned into stars to escape a hunter. He tells me about constellations and planets and galaxies. He tells me about the moon landing, about Neil Armstrong's first steps, about how humans had reached out and touched another world.

"It changed everything for me," he says quietly. "Made me realize how small we are. How insignificant, really, in the grand scheme of things. But also, how amazing. That we're here at all, that we get to see this..." he gestures at the sky "it's kind of a miracle, you know?"

I think about that. About being small and insignificant but also miraculous.

"I like feeling small," I say. "When you're small, you're harder to see. And when you can't be seen..." I trail off, not quite able to finish the thought. But David seems to understand.

"Yeah. I know what you mean."

But I'm not sure he does.

Without thinking, I move closer to him, resting my head on his shoulder.

He goes still for a moment, then wraps his arm around me, pulling me in close.

"Is this okay?" I ask.

"Yeah," he says, his voice rough. "This is okay."

We lie there like that, my head on his shoulder, his arm around me, watching the stars wheel slowly overhead. I feel safe here, in the middle of nowhere, with this man I barely know but who seems to understand me in ways I don't understand myself.

A shooting star streaks across the sky, bright and brief.

"Did you see that?" I whisper.

"Yeah. Make a wish."

I close my eyes and wish for this feeling to last. This peace. This safety. This freedom.

When I open them again, a bird, some kind of night bird, flies overhead, its silhouette dark against the stars. I watch it until it disappears into the darkness.

"Thank you," I say to David.

"For what?"

"For this. For stopping. For..." I don't know how to finish the sentence. For seeing me? For understanding? For being kind?

"You don't have to thank me," he says. "I wanted to do this. Wanted to show you... this." He gestures at the sky again. "All of this. The world. There's so much of it, Mary. So much more than you've seen."

His words make something twist in my chest. More than I've seen. As if I've been somewhere small, somewhere confined. But I can't quite grasp what he means, can't quite hold onto the thought.

"Will you tell me more?" I ask. "About the stars? About space?"

"All night if you want," he says.

So he does. He talks about black holes and supernovas and the expanding universe. He talks about light years and time dilation and the possibility of other worlds, other lives. His voice is soft and steady, and I listen to it mixing with the sound of my own breathing, with the occasional rustle of some small creature in the scrub, with the vast silence of the Nullarbor night.

Eventually, his voice starts to fade, becoming distant, dreamlike. My eyelids grow heavy.

"You should sleep," David murmurs. "Long day tomorrow."

"Mmm." I'm already half-gone, drifting.

The last thing I'm aware of is David pulling the blanket over both of us, his arm still around me, holding me close. Above us, the stars shine on, infinite and indifferent and beautiful.

I don't think about tomorrow. I don't think about yesterday. There's only now, this moment, this sky, this feeling of being held.

Chapter 4

David woke to the sound of birdsong and the cool grey light of dawn. For a moment, he didn't move, just lay there with Mary's weight against his shoulder, her breathing soft and even. She was still asleep; one hand curled loosely against his chest. Peaceful.

He hadn't slept much. Every time he'd started to drift off, some small sound would jolt him awake, a rustle in the scrub, the distant howl of a dingo, the settling of the cooling earth. And each time, his first instinct was to check that Mary was still there, still breathing, still present.

She was. For now.

Carefully, David extracted himself from beneath her, easing her head onto the folded blanket. She stirred slightly but didn't wake. He stood, his back aching from a night on hard ground, and looked out at the landscape around them.

The Nullarbor stretched out in all directions, vast and empty and painted in shades of grey and pink by the rising sun. It was beautiful, in its way. Desolate, but beautiful. The kind of place where a person could disappear entirely and never be found.

The thought made David's stomach clench.

He walked a little distance from the car to relieve himself, then dug through his bag for the snack bars and water bottles he'd packed. As he moved, he found himself thinking about Mary, about how they'd met, about how far they'd come.

Almost a year now. She'd been so fragile at first, so uncertain. But gradually she'd opened up to him, let him in. He'd fallen for her completely, for her gentleness, her wonder at simple things, her desperate need for freedom.

When the Adelaide job came through, it had seemed like fate. A fresh start for both of them. A chance to leave everything behind and begin again.

He'd been careful planning this trip. Made sure she had everything she needed. Made sure she'd be safe. He just wanted to give her this, a chance at a normal life, away from everything that had hurt her before.

But the episodes worried him. The times when she'd lose track of time, forget things, seem confused about where she was or what year it was. Yesterday at the motel had scared him, waking up to find her gone, finding her on the roadside not remembering him at all.

Still, she'd seemed better last night. Peaceful under the stars. Like maybe this was working. Like maybe they'd be okay.

He walked back to where she lay sleeping. Her face was peaceful, almost childlike. The red polka dot dress was wrinkled and dusty, her white boots lying beside the blanket where she'd kicked them off in the night.

David knelt down and gently shook her shoulder. "Mary. Hey. Time to wake up."

She stirred, eyes fluttering open. For a moment, she looked confused, that brief, disoriented expression everyone has when waking somewhere unfamiliar. Then she focused on him and smiled.

"Good morning," she said.

"Morning. Sleep okay?"

"Yes." She sat up, looking around at the empty landscape. "We're really in the middle of nowhere, aren't we?"

"Yeah. We are." He handed her a water bottle. "Drink some of this. And here..."

He pulled out the tin of peppermints, shaking out one of the white tablets. "Have your morning candy."

She took it without question, swallowing it with a gulp of water. Good. That was good.

They packed up quickly, folding the blanket, loading everything back into the boot. The sun was fully up now, already starting to heat the day. David estimated they had another full day of driving ahead of them, maybe more.

"Ready?" he asked.

"Ready," Mary said, climbing into the passenger seat.

They merged back onto the highway, the Volvo's engine humming steadily. For a while, neither of them spoke. Mary had her arm out the window again, eyes half-closed, that peaceful expression on her face.

David found himself relaxing slightly. Maybe it would be okay. Maybe they'd make it to Adelaide without any more episodes. Maybe...

A figure appeared on the road ahead. A man, standing on the shoulder with his thumb out, a dark green duffle bag at his feet.

David's first instinct was to drive past. They didn't need complications. Didn't need anyone else involved in this mess.

But as they got closer, he could see the man more clearly, stocky build, short hair, moustache. Military posture. And something about the way he stood there, patient and hopeful, made David think of all the times he'd been the one hitching, the one hoping for kindness from strangers.

Before he could fully think it through, David was slowing down, pulling over.

"What are you doing?" Mary asked.

"Picking up a hitchhiker," David said. "It's a long, empty road. We should help."

Mary looked uncertain but didn't protest.

The back door opened, and the man climbed in, duffle bag and all. He had a weathered face, probably late twenties or early thirties, with tired eyes that had seen too much.

"Thanks for stopping, brother," he said. His accent was American—Southern. "Where are you headed?"

"Adelaide," David said. "Where do you want to be, man?"

"Adelaide sounds great to me too," the stranger said. He settled into the back seat with a sigh of relief. "Name's James. It's a pleasure to meet you."

"James, I'm David. And this is Mary," David said, nodding toward Mary in the passenger seat.

"Ma'am," James said, tipping an imaginary hat. "It's a pleasure to meet you too."

Mary turned in her seat to look at him. David caught the expression on her face, curious, but also something else. Wary, maybe. Or confused.

"Why are you here?" she asked. Not rudely, just genuinely curious.

"Well ma'am, I was in 'Nam, and I got a bit disillusioned about going back home, with all the protests an all. Thought I'd travel your fine country instead."

Mary's eyes widened. "'Nam? You've travelled a lot. I want to travel too. Tell me about this 'Nam place."

James chuckled, but there was no humour in it. "Ma'am, my stories are not ones to be told to fine ladies like yourself."

Mary looked confused. David leaned over and whispered, "He's talking about the Vietnam war."

She nodded slowly, but her expression remained confused, like she'd never heard of it. Or like she had but couldn't quite place it.

David and James started talking, about the road, about Australia, about Adelaide. James had an easy way about him, the kind of man who'd learned to make friends quickly in unfamiliar places. David found himself relaxing into the conversation, grateful for the company.

In the passenger seat, Mary had gone quiet. She stared out the windscreen, her arm hanging out in the wind, but her expression was distant now. Troubled.

David glanced at her, concerned, but didn't want to ask if she was okay in front of James. So, he just kept driving, kept talking, and watched the road stretch out ahead of them into the shimmering heat.

Chapter 5

I wake to David's voice calling my name softly, his hand on my shoulder. For a moment I'm confused, the sky above me, the blanket beneath me, the vast emptiness all around. Then I remember. The road. Adelaide. David.

"Good morning," I say, smiling up at him.

"Morning. Sleep okay?"

"Yes." I sit up, looking around at the beautiful desolation. We really did sleep under the stars. It feels like a dream, but a good one.

David hands me a water bottle and then that little tin of peppermints. I take one without thinking about it, swallowing it down. My morning routine. David always gives me one in the morning and one at night. Says they're good for me.

As we pack up the blanket and get ready to go, I find myself thinking about how I got here. How David and I met.

It was at the shop. Mother's shop, really—the little boutique in Mosman Park where she used to work before she died. I'd taken it over, or maybe the house staff had arranged for me to work there. I can't quite remember how it started. But I remember standing behind the counter in my polka dot dress, arranging stock, and David walking in one day.

He'd seemed so out of place among the women's clothes and accessories. But he'd smiled at me, that warm, gentle smile, and asked if we sold anything for his sister. We didn't have a sister's section, but I'd helped him anyway, picking out a scarf I thought might be nice.

He'd come back the next week. And the week after that. Each time with some excuse, looking for a gift, needing advice, just passing by. But really, I think he was coming to see me.

We'd talk for hours when the shop was quiet. He'd tell me about his dreams of working for the Space Agency, about Adelaide, about wanting to start fresh. And I'd tell him about wanting to travel, to see the world beyond Mosman Park, beyond the big house by the river where I lived with the staff.

Eventually, he'd asked me to come with him. To Adelaide. To start a new life.

I'd been terrified. I'd never been away from home before. Never had to take care of myself. At the house, the staff did everything, the cooking, cleaning, making sure I was where I needed to be, helping me when I got confused about things. How would I manage on my own?

But David had promised he'd take care of me. That we'd take care of each other.

So I'd asked for the weekend off from the shop. Packed my small suitcase. Put on my favourite dress and boots. And met him at the arranged spot.

Or had I? The memory feels slippery somehow, like it's not quite solid. Did we leave from the shop? Or from the house? Did I tell the staff I was leaving, or did I just go?

"You okay?" David asks, watching me from where he's loading the last of our things into the boot.

"Yes," I say quickly. "Just thinking."

"About what?"

"About Adelaide. About starting over." I hesitate. "Do you think I'll be able to manage? Without... without help?"

Something flickers across his face, concern, maybe, or sadness. "You'll be fine. We'll figure it out together."

"But I've always had people to help me. The staff at the house, they..."

"Mary," he says gently, coming over to me. "You're stronger than you think. You just need a chance to prove it to yourself."

I want to believe him. I do believe him, mostly. But there's this nagging doubt, this sense that I'm forgetting something important.

"Ready to hit the road?" he asks.

I nod, climbing into the passenger seat. The familiar smell of the car, vinyl and coffee and David, settles around me like a comfort.

We drive for a while in comfortable silence. I watch the landscape pass, my arm out the window, feeling the wind. A magpie swoops low across the road ahead of us, black and white against the blue sky. I watch until it disappears.

Then David speaks, breaking my reverie. "So I was thinking... when we get to Adelaide, first thing we should do is get you some new clothes. Something more... modern, you know? Not that you don't look great, but..."

"What's wrong with my clothes?" I look down at my polka dot dress. It's one of my favourites. Mother helped me pick it out, I think. Or maybe I picked it out myself?

"Nothing's wrong with them," David says quickly. "They're groovy. I just meant, you know, for job interviews and stuff. Adelaide's a bit more... 1977 than Perth."

That number again. It still doesn't feel right in my mouth.

"What year do you think it is?" David asks carefully.

I open my mouth to answer, then close it. I don't know. The numbers slip away from me every time I try to hold onto them.

"Does it matter?" I ask instead.

"No," he says after a moment. "No, I guess it doesn't."

We drive on. The sun climbs higher. The heat builds. And then, in the back seat...

I turn around and there's a man sitting there. Dark green duffle bag beside him, stocky build, moustache. How long has he been there? I nearly jump out of my seat.

"Thanks for stopping, brother," the man says to David. "Where are you headed?"

"Adelaide," David says. "Where do you want to be, man?"

My heart is hammering. When did we stop? When did we pick him up? I don't remember stopping.

"Adelaide sounds great to me too," the man says. He looks at me and smiles. "Name's James. It's a pleasure to meet you, ma'am."

"James, I'm David. And this is Mary," David says, like this is all perfectly normal.

"Ma'am," James says again, tipping an imaginary hat at me.

I stare at him. There's something about him, something familiar but wrong. Something that makes my stomach twist.

"Why are you here?" I hear myself ask.

"Well ma'am, I was in 'Nam, and I got a bit disillusioned about going back home, with all the protests an all. Thought I'd travel your fine country instead."

'Nam. Vietnam. The word hits me like a physical thing. My father...

No. I push the thought away before it can fully form.

"You've travelled a lot," I say, trying to keep my voice steady. "I want to travel too. Tell me about this 'Nam place."

"Ma'am, my stories are not ones to be told to fine ladies like yourself."

David leans over, whispers to me: "He's talking about the Vietnam war."

The Vietnam war. My father was in the Vietnam war. My father...

I turn back to face forward, gripping the door handle. My breathing is too fast. The voices behind me, David and James talking, laughing fade into background noise, mixing with the wind, with the hum of the engine, with the static that's always there at the edges of my hearing.

I stick my arm out the window and close my eyes. Pretend I'm flying. Pretend I'm anywhere but here, with a stranger who reminds me of things I don't want to remember.

When you're small, you're harder to see. And when you can't be seen, bad things can't find you.

I repeat it to myself like a mantra as the car carries us forward, deeper into the Nullarbor, further from everything I know.

I am small. I am invisible. I am safe.

But even as I think it, I know it's a lie.

Chapter 6

The voices behind me blur together, David's easy laugh, James's drawling accent, words I can't quite catch. I keep my arm out the window, eyes closed, but I can't shake the feeling of being watched.

I adjust the side mirror slightly, angling it so I can see into the back seat without turning around. James is sitting there, relaxed, one arm draped over his duffle bag. He's looking out his window, but every so often his eyes flick forward, catching mine in the mirror.

When he does, he smiles. A friendly smile. A warm smile.

But all I see are the eyes. Dark eyes. Watching eyes. Eyes that followed me through the house when I was small, tracking my movements from room to room. Eyes that would appear in doorways. In mirrors. In the dark.

"That's a real nice dress you're wearing, ma'am," James says, his voice friendly, just trying to make conversation. "The polka dots are real pretty."

I look at him in the mirror. "Thank you, it's your favourite," I say, giving a little smile, trying to please him.

Then I turn back to the window immediately, making myself smaller in the seat.

In the back, James blinks, confused. He glances at David.

David catches his eye and just gives a small shake of his head, then launches into a story about the road ahead, smoothly redirecting the conversation.

I look away quickly, my heart racing.

The hum of the car, the heat, the endless sameness of the landscape, it all starts to press down on me. My eyelids grow heavy. I try to fight it, but exhaustion pulls at me like a weight.

I drift.

***

The door to my room creaks open. I'm twelve, maybe thirteen. It's late, I can tell by the quality of darkness outside my window, by the silence of the house.

"Mary?" His voice is rough. Slurred. "You awake, Mary?"

I don't answer. If I'm very still, very quiet, very small, maybe he'll think I'm asleep. Maybe he'll go away.

"I know you're awake."

The smell hits me first, Old Spice cologne and cigarette smoke and something else, something wrong. The bed dips as he sits down.

"Your mother would have wanted me to check on you. Make sure you're okay."

Mother's been gone for months. But I don't say that. I don't say anything.

His hand on my shoulder. Heavy. Too heavy.

"You're a good girl, aren't you Mary? You take care of your old man?"

I squeeze my eyes shut tighter. Make myself smaller. So small I might disappear completely.

"Look at me when I'm talking to you."

I don't want to look. But I do. And there they are, those eyes. Dark and empty and watching. Always watching.

"That's my girl."

***

I jerk awake, gasping. The car is still moving. David is still talking to James. Nothing has changed.

But my heart is hammering and there's sweat on my forehead despite the wind from the window.

I glance at the side mirror again. James is looking right at me. He smiles.

Those eyes. The same eyes.

No. No, that's not right. James isn't my father. My father is... where is my father? Dead, I think. He's dead. Isn't he?

"You alright there, ma'am?" James asks from the back seat. His voice is kind. Concerned.

I can't answer. My throat has closed up.

"Mary?" David glances at me. "You look pale. You need me to pull over?"

I shake my head quickly. "No. I'm fine. Just... dozed off for a minute."

But I'm not fine. Every time I look in that mirror, every time I catch James's eyes, I see something else. Someone else.

The rational part of my brain knows this is wrong. Knows James is just a hitchhiker, a stranger, a veteran trying to get to Adelaide. Knows he hasn't done anything to me.

But the other part, the part that remembers the weight on the bed, the hand on my shoulder, the eyes in the dark, that part can't tell the difference.

I adjust the mirror again, angling it away so I can't see him anymore. But I can still feel him there, right behind me, watching.

David and James keep talking. Something about cars, about the Volvo's engine, about the road ahead. Normal conversation. Safe conversation.

But underneath it, I hear something else. A whisper, maybe. Or a memory.

"You're a good girl, aren't you Mary?"

I put my arm back out the window and close my eyes again, I need to escape, to fly away. This time I don't drift. I stay alert, awake, aware of every sound behind me.

The road stretches on. The heat builds. And in the back seat, James shifts position, and I hear the rustle of his jacket against the seat.

Just a rustle. Just fabric.

But it sounds like a door creaking open in the dark.

I count my breaths. One. Two. Three. Try to slow my racing heart.

I shift in my seat, pulling my knees up slightly, trying to make myself smaller. If I curl up just right, maybe I'll take up less space. Maybe I won't be so visible. Maybe those eyes in the mirror won't find me.

David glances over. "You comfortable?"

"Yes," I lie.

I tuck myself tighter against the door, my arm still out the window but my body folded in on itself. Small. Invisible. Safe. The words repeat in my head like a prayer that's never answered.

We're just driving to Adelaide. That's all. Just David and me and a hitchhiker. Nothing bad is happening. Nothing bad is going to happen.

But I can't make myself believe it.

"How much further to the next town?" I hear myself ask, my voice too high, too tight.

"Few hours yet," David says. "Why? You need to stop?"

"No. Just wondering."

Few hours. Few more hours with those eyes behind me. Few more hours of trying to stay small, stay invisible, stay safe.

I watch a hawk circling overhead, so high it's barely a speck. Free. Untouchable. Beyond reach.

That's what I want to be.

But instead I'm here, trapped in this car with my fragmented memories and a stranger who isn't my father but might as well be, heading toward a future I can't quite picture, running from a past I can't quite remember.

But the past is right here with me. It's in the back seat, watching me in the mirror, smiling with friendly eyes that aren't friendly at all.

The mirror catches my eye again. I'd angled it away, but somehow, it's shifted. And there he is, James, looking right at me. Smiling that friendly smile.

But the eyes. The eyes are all wrong.

I turn to face forward and don't look back again.

Chapter 7

David had been watching Mary out of the corner of his eye for the past hour, growing more concerned with each passing minute. She'd curled herself up against the passenger door like a wounded animal trying to make itself small. Her knees were drawn up, her body twisted in a way that couldn't possibly be comfortable, but when he'd asked if she was okay, she'd just said yes in that too-bright voice that meant she was anything but.

He should have known this would happen. Should have anticipated it. James mentioning Vietnam, talking about the war, of course that would trigger something in Mary. Her father had been a vet. Had come back broken and violent and had taken it all out on her.

But what could David do now? Tell James to stop talking? Explain that Mary had trauma related to Vietnam veterans? That would require explaining Mary's whole situation, and he couldn't do that. Not without her permission. Not without risking everything.

So he just kept driving and kept up his end of the conversation with James, talking about Australia and Adelaide and anything except the war, while Mary made herself smaller and smaller in the seat beside him.

"You thinking of settling in Adelaide permanently?" James was asking. "Or just passing through?"

"Settling," David said. "Got a job lined up at the Australian Space Agency. Engineering work. Starts in January."

"No kidding? That's far out, man. Working on rockets and satellites and all that?"

"Something like that, yeah."

"And your lady there..." James nodded toward Mary "she got work lined up too?"

David glanced at Mary. She was staring straight ahead, arms wrapped around her knees, completely shut down. "We'll figure that out when we get there," he said carefully.

James must have picked up on something in his tone because he didn't press further. Instead, he started talking about his own plans—maybe find work on a sheep station, or head up north to the mines, or just keep traveling and see where the road took him.

David made appropriate noises of interest, but his attention was split. Part of him was in the conversation, part of him was watching Mary, and part of him was doing the mental math on how much further they had to go.

Another full day of driving, at least. Maybe more if they hit any delays. And then what? Would Mary be okay once they got to Adelaide? Would getting away from everything finally help her heal, or would she just...

Thud.

Thud thud thud thud.

"Ah, shit," David muttered, feeling the distinctive wobble of a flat tire. He eased off the accelerator, guiding the Volvo toward the shoulder.

"What a bummer, man," he said, more to himself than to his passengers. "I think we've got a flat tire."

He pulled over completely and cut the engine. The sudden silence was stark after hours of road noise and conversation.

Mary's head snapped up. "Where are we?"

"This is the Nullarbor," David said. "There's nothing here for miles around, except for the ocean, just over there." He pointed out his window toward the cliff line visible a few hundred meters away.

Mary's eyes went wide. "I have to see it. I want to see it."

Before David could respond, she was scrambling out of the car, her earlier paralysis forgotten in sudden manic energy.

"Mary, wait!" David called after her, but she was already running toward the ocean, her red dress bright against the scrubland.

"Ok, baby," he said to himself, then louder: "But you take care out there, it can be a dangerous place!"

She didn't seem to hear him. Just kept running.

David sighed and climbed out of the car. James was already standing by the back, looking after Mary with a bemused expression.

"She really wanted to see that ocean," James observed.

"Yeah. She's been cooped up for a while. Not much freedom to just... run, you know?"

James nodded slowly, and David wondered if he'd revealed too much. But James just said, "I'll give you a hand changing the wheel, sir."

"Cool, man," David said, genuinely grateful. "I've just got to get my things out of the boot first."

He opened the boot and started pulling out bags to get to the spare tire and jack underneath. As he worked, he kept glancing toward where Mary had disappeared over a small rise. She'd be okay for a bit. Let her have her moment with the ocean. God knows she deserved it.

The spare tire was in good shape; he'd checked it before they left. The jack was there, the wrench, everything they needed. David and James worked in companionable silence, loosening the lug nuts on the flat tire, jacking up the car, pulling off the damaged wheel.

"Looks like you ran over some debris," James said, examining the flat. "Got a nasty gash right here."

"At least it's just the one," David said. "And at least it happened out here where we could pull over safely. Imagine if it had blown on a curve or something."

"You got that right."

They got the spare on and tightened down. The whole process took maybe twenty minutes, thirty at most. David stood up, wiping his hands on his jeans, and looked toward the ocean again.

Mary still wasn't back.

"I'm going to put my things back in the boot," David said. "Maybe you could go check on her? Let her know we're ready to go?"

"Sure thing," James said, already starting toward the direction Mary had gone.

David watched him go for a moment, then turned his attention back to the car. He loaded the flat tire into the boot, reorganized the bags, made sure everything was secure. Took his time, giving Mary those extra minutes by the ocean. She'd been so tense in the car, so wound up. Maybe the space and the view would help calm her down.

He was just closing the boot when he heard it.

A scream. Faint, distant, but unmistakable.

David's blood turned to ice.

"Mary!"

He took off running, his heart hammering. Images flooded his mind, Mary slipping off the cliff, James startling her, something going wrong. He'd seen the way James kept looking at her in the rearview mirror. Those smiles. Had David been wrong to trust him? Had he just sent a stranger to find his vulnerable, traumatized...

Another sound. A shout this time. Male voice.

James.

David ran faster, his breath coming in gasps. The scrub tore at his jeans. Rocks turned under his feet, but he didn't slow down. Thoughts raced through his head, each one worse than the last.

If he's touched her. If he's hurt her. If he's done anything!

I'll kill him. I'll fucking kill him.

He crested the rise and saw the cliff ahead. Mary, standing near the edge, alone.

But where was James?

David slowed his approach, his eyes scanning the area. "Mary! Where's James?"

She turned to look at him, and the expression on her face made his stomach drop. Terror. Pure, absolute terror.

"Mary, what happened?" David moved closer, his voice urgent. "Are you okay? Where's James?"

She didn't answer. Just stared at him with those wide, frightened eyes.

David reached the cliff edge and looked down.

James's body was sprawled across the rocks below, twisted at an impossible angle. Blood. So much blood.

"Oh my god," David breathed. "Oh my god, no."

He spun back to Mary. "What happened? Did he fall? Did you see?"

But she just kept staring at him with that look of absolute horror, backing toward the edge.

"Mary, stop!" David lunged forward and grabbed her shoulders, trying to pull her away from the crumbling cliff edge. "It's okay. You're okay. Just come away from there."

"What did you do? What did you do?" Mary was shouting now, thrashing in his grip.

"Mary, it's me. It's David. I'm not going to hurt you." He kept his hands on her shoulders, firm but gentle, trying to guide her away from the danger. "Just come with me. Come back to the car. Everything's going to be alright."

"Get off me!" She was fighting him now, really fighting, her whole body twisting and writhing.

David tried to hold on, tried to move her back from the edge, but she was surprisingly strong in her panic. They stumbled together, feet tangling. Mary lost her balance and fell backward, pulling David down with her.

They hit the ground hard. Mary underneath, David falling on top of her, trying to catch himself.

"Mary, please..." he started to say, trying to get up, trying not to crush her.

But she was screaming now, hysterical. "Get off me! Get off me!"

David tried to push himself up, to give her space, but in her panic, Mary brought her knee up hard. It caught him square in the groin.

White-hot pain exploded through David's body. He rolled off her, gasping, clutching himself, unable to breathe or think or do anything except curl up in agony.

Through the haze of pain, he heard Mary scrambling to her feet. Heard her running.

"Mary... wait..." he managed to gasp out, but she was already gone.

David lay there for a moment, trying to get his breath back, trying to make the pain subside enough that he could move. Finally, he forced himself onto his hands and knees, then to his feet.

Mary was running toward the car.

"Mary! Stop!" David staggered after her, still bent over, one hand pressed to his groin. "Please! You don't understand!"

She reached the car and threw herself into the driver's seat.

"No, no, no," David muttered, forcing himself to run despite the pain. "Mary, you can't drive. You don't..."

The engine started.

David ran faster. He could see her through the windscreen, her face streaked with blood, when had that happened? Her hands fumbling with the gearshift.

The car lurched backward. Mary's head snapped forward, hitting the steering wheel. More blood.

"Mary!" David shouted.

The car screeched to a stop.

David threw his hands up, his face pleading. "Mary, please! Stop! It's me!"

And then...

She smiled.

Relief flooded through David so intensely his knees nearly buckled. She recognised him. She understood.

Everything was going to be okay.

Chapter 8

I run toward the ocean, my feet pounding against the red earth, my dress whipping around my legs. Behind me, the car, the road, the voices, they all fade away. Ahead of me, just the cliff and the sky and the beautiful, terrible emptiness.

I have to get away from those eyes. Those watching, waiting eyes.

The cliff edge appears suddenly, and I stop just short of it, my breath coming in gasps. Below, the ocean crashes against the rocks in explosions of white foam. The sound is enormous, drowning out everything else, the static in my head, the whispers, the memories.

I stand there mesmerized, watching the waves. The power of them. The way they just keep coming, relentless, breaking themselves against the rocks over and over.

The wind whips my hair across my face. Seabirds wheel overhead, their cries sharp and lonely. I watch them, following their patterns against the blue.

Free. They're free.

Time does something strange. Slips sideways. I'm standing at the cliff, and then I'm not sure how long I've been standing here. Minutes? Hours? The sun hasn't moved much, but my legs ache like I've been still for a long time.

I should go back to the car. David will be worried.

But I can't make myself move. Something about this spot, this exact piece of ground, it feels important. Like something happened here. Or is going to happen. Or is happening right now in a way I can't quite see.

Footsteps behind me.

I spin around.

James is walking toward me, his duffle bag left somewhere behind him. He's smiling that friendly smile, but all I see are the eyes. Dark. Watching. Coming closer.

"Quite a view, isn't it, ma'am?" he says.

I take a step back. My heel finds the edge of the cliff. Loose rocks skitter down into the void.

"Don't get too close to the edge there," James says, still approaching. "Dangerous spot."

But he's the dangerous one. I know he is. I've seen those eyes before.

"Stay back," I hear myself say.

He stops, holds up his hands. "Hey, it's okay. David just sent me to let you know the car's fixed. We're ready to go."

David. The name feels distant, like something from another life. But this, this man in front of me with the dark eyes and the smile that doesn't reach them, this is familiar in a way that makes my skin crawl.

"I know what you are," I say.

James looks confused. "Ma'am, I think maybe the sun's got to you. Why don't we head back?"

He takes a step closer.

And suddenly I'm not at the cliff anymore. I'm in my room. I'm twelve years old. The door is opening. The smell of whiskey and cigarettes. The weight on the bed. The hand on my shoulder.

"You're a good girl, aren't you Mary?"

"No," I whisper. "No, not again. Not again."

"Mary?" James sounds concerned now. "Are you okay?"

He reaches out toward me.

And I?

The memory swallows me whole. I'm not here. I'm there. I'm twelve and fourteen and ten and eight and every age I ever was when the door opened and he came in. Every time I made myself small. Every time I tried to disappear. Every time it didn't work.

"Look at me when I'm talking to you."

I look at James, but I don't see James. I see my father. I see those eyes. The eyes that followed me. The eyes that found me even when I hid. The eyes that watched and waited and...

"Stay away from me!" I'm shouting now, backing up. The cliff edge is right behind me, but I don't care. "Don't touch me! Don't you dare touch me!"

"Mary, I'm not..." James holds up his hands, trying to calm me. "I'm not going to hurt you. I just..."

But he's coming closer. One step. Two steps. Just like before. Just like always.

Time fragments. I'm here and I'm not here. I'm at the cliff and I'm in my room and I'm everywhere I've ever been afraid.

James is saying something but I can't hear it over the roaring in my ears. The ocean? My pulse? The static that's always there, always waiting?

He's close now. Too close. Reaching out.

And I.

I push.

Or do I?

The memory is confused. Fractured. There's a movement, mine or his, I can't tell. There's a scream, mine or his, I can't tell. There's a moment where everything hangs suspended, where James's eyes go wide with surprise or fear or something else.

And then he's not there anymore.

Just empty space where he was standing.

And a sound. A terrible, final sound from below.

I stand frozen, staring at the spot where he was. The wind keeps blowing. The ocean keeps crashing. The birds keep crying overhead.

Did that happen?

Did I do that?

I move to the edge on shaking legs and look down.

James is there. On the rocks. Not moving. The dark green of his jacket stark against the grey stone. Red spreading out from underneath him, mixing with the sea spray.

My stomach lurches. I stumble back from the edge.

No. No, that's not right. That didn't happen. James fell. He got too close to the edge and he fell. I didn't, I wouldn't!

But I did. Didn't I?

The memory is already rewriting itself, smoothing over the rough edges, filling in the gaps with something more bearable. He slipped. He lost his balance. It was an accident. I was nowhere near him.

But my hands. Why are my hands shaking? Why does my chest feel like it's being crushed?

A sound behind me. Footsteps. Running.

I turn.

David is there, running toward me, his face pale and frightened.

And behind him...

No. Wait. There's no one behind him. James is down on the rocks. James is gone.

But for just a second, I could swear I saw someone else. Those same eyes. Watching. Following.

Always following.

"Mary!" David shouts. "Where's James?"

I can't answer. My throat has closed up. My whole body is shaking.

David reaches the edge and looks down. I watch his face change, shock, horror, disbelief.

"Oh my god," he breathes. "Oh my god, no."

He spins back to me. "What happened? Did he fall? Did you see?"

Did I see?

I was there. I was right there. But the memory keeps slipping away, keeps rewriting itself. James slipped. No, I pushed. No, he fell. No, I...

He grabs my shoulders. "What did you do? What did you do?"

His face is right in mine now. His eyes, those eyes. I know those eyes.

And suddenly I understand. It's not David. It never was David. It's been him all along. My father. Following me. Finding me even here, even in the middle of nowhere.

"Come here," he says, and his voice is different now. Rough. Eager.

No. No, not again.

"I wasn't asking!" he shouts when I try to pull away.

His grip on my shoulders tightens, fingers digging in hard enough to bruise. His face so close I can smell him, sweat and something else, something wrong.

"Do you know how much of a turn on that was?" he says, his eyes flicking toward the cliff edge, toward where James fell. "Watching you do that?"

I'm frozen. Can't move. Can't breathe. Just like before. Always like before.

"Don't," I whisper. "Please don't."

But he's not listening. He never listened. His mouth crashes onto mine, his tongue forcing its way between my lips. One hand leaves my shoulder, moves down to grab at my breast through the thin fabric of my dress.

I can't, I can't!

He pushes me down. I hit the ground hard, my back slamming against the earth, knees bent up. I see his hands moving to his belt, see him kneeling at my feet.

"This one will be the best one yet!" he says, reaching for my underwear.

No. Not this time. Never again.

"Stop! Stop!" I'm screaming now, hysteria clawing its way up my throat. Tears pour down my face.

He doesn't stop. He's pulling at my clothes, climbing over me.

"Get off me! Get off me!" I scream at the top of my lungs, wriggling, fighting, trying to free myself.

"Come here, baby, you know you like it," he says.

Something inside me snaps. Pure animal panic. Pure survival instinct.

I bring my knee up hard, as hard as I can, straight into his groin.

He makes a terrible sound, half gasp, half wheeze, and crumples to the side.

I don't think. Don't hesitate. Don't look back.

I scramble to my feet and run.

Behind me, I hear him shouting, calling after me, his voice ragged with pain and rage. But I don't stop. I run like I should have run years ago. Run like my life depends on it.

Because it does.

The car. I need the car. Need to get away.

I throw myself into the driver's seat. My hands are shaking so badly I can barely get the key in the ignition. Behind me, I hear him, Father, shouting my name.

"Mary! Come back here! Mary!"

No. Never. Not anymore.

The engine starts. I put it in gear. Press the accelerator.

The car lurches backward. My head smacks into the steering wheel. Pain explodes across my forehead. Blood runs down into my eyes. Everything is red and blurred and spinning.

Brakes. Forward. Accelerator.

The car shoots forward just as he appears in front of it, Father, bent over, one hand clutching his groin, the other reaching out toward me.

I don't have time to think. Don't have time to stop. Don't have time to do anything except watch his legs buckle as the car hits him, watch him fly up onto the bonnet, watch his face smash into the windscreen, watch his nose explode in a spray of blood, watch his body roll up and over the roof and off the back.

And then he's gone.

In the rearview mirror, I see him lying in the dust.

Not moving.

I keep driving.

I have to keep driving.

Father is dead. Father is finally dead.

I killed him.

I killed my own father.

The thought should horrify me, but all I feel is a strange, hollow relief. It's over. It's finally over.

The further away I get, the less it happened.

That's how it works. That's how it's always worked.

If I drive far enough, fast enough, maybe none of it will be real.

Maybe I'll wake up in my room at Greenplace and it will all have been a dream.

Maybe Mother will be singing downstairs.

Maybe the door will stay closed tonight.

Maybe I'll be safe.

I drive into the empty heart of the Nullarbor, and behind me, my father lies broken on the red earth, bleeding into the dust.

But it doesn't matter how far I drive.

Because even though he's dead now, even though I finally stopped him, I know the truth.

The past is already inside me.

And it's been there all along.

Chapter 9

The steering wheel is slick with blood. My blood, I think, though I'm not entirely sure anymore. Everything is red, the dust on the windscreen, the sunset bleeding across the horizon, the sticky warmth running down my face.

I keep driving.

Father taught me how to drive. The memory surfaces unbidden, unwanted. I was ten, maybe eleven. Before everything got really bad. He'd take me out to the outback, empty roads where no one would see, and let me sit on his lap behind the steering wheel.

"Keep your eyes on the road, Mary," he'd say, his breath warm against my ear. "Hands at ten and two. That's my girl."

His hands would be on top of mine on the wheel, guiding. Teaching.

And then one hand would slip away. Down. Under.

"Eyes on the road, Mary. Don't look away. Keep driving."

I'd kept my eyes on the road. Always kept my eyes on the road. Because if I looked, if I acknowledged what was happening, it would become real. And if it was real, I'd have to do something about it. And I couldn't. I was too small. Too afraid.

So I'd just kept driving.

Just like I'm doing now.

Other memories surface, jostling for space. Father lifting me onto his shoulders to see the Christmas lights. "You're my special girl, Mary. My special, special girl." Special. That word always meant something different when he said it.

Father and Mother dancing in the kitchen, Sinatra on the record player. Mother laughing, flour on her nose from baking. Father twirling her, and for that moment, just that moment, he was the man she'd married. The man before the war. Before Vietnam broke something inside him that never healed.

But then Mother would go to bed, and Father would stay up drinking, and the door to my room would creak open in the dark.

"Mary? You awake?"

I'd always pretend to be asleep. Make myself small. Try to make myself invisible.

It never worked.

"I know you're awake, Mary. Don't pretend with me."

Good Father. Bad Father. Sometimes I couldn't tell which one would appear. The one who taught me to ride a bike and cheered when I stayed upright. Or the one who came to my room at night with whiskey on his breath and something broken in his eyes.

Maybe they were always the same person. Maybe I just wanted to believe there were two, because one man being capable of both love and horror was too much to comprehend.

The Nullarbor stretches out ahead of me, endless and empty. The road is a grey line cutting through red earth, disappearing into the heat shimmer. No other cars. No signs of life. Just me and the broken windscreen and the hum of the engine and these memories I can't escape.

Hours pass. Or maybe minutes. Time has lost all meaning.

The sun sinks lower, painting the sky in shades of orange and purple. Beautiful. It's so beautiful it makes my chest hurt. Or maybe that's something else. Maybe that's the weight of what I've done pressing down on me, making it hard to breathe.

Father is dead.

I killed him.

The words repeat in my head like a mantra, like a song, like the static from the radio that's blessedly silent now. Father is dead. I killed him. Father is dead. I killed him.

Should I feel guilty? Should I feel sorry?

All I feel is numb.

And tired. So, so tired.

My hands are cramping from gripping the steering wheel. My head throbs where I hit it. Every time I blink, the world takes a second too long to come back into focus.

A bird, some kind of hawk or eagle, flies alongside the car for a moment, keeping pace. I watch it through the cracked windscreen. It's so effortless, the way it moves. Wings barely moving, just riding the air currents.

I wanted to be like that. Free like that.

Am I free now?

The bird veers off, disappearing into the darkening sky.

The sun finally sets completely, and darkness swallows the world. The Volvo's single working headlight cuts a weak path through the black. The other one must have smashed when Father... when the accident... when...

I can't think about it.

Keep driving. Just keep driving.

The road becomes hypnotic. White line, grey tarmac, red earth. White line, grey tarmac, red earth. Over and over. My eyelids grow heavy. I force them open. Can't stop. Can't sleep. If I stop, if I sleep, it all becomes real.

Sometime in the deep night, I pass a sign: PORT AUGUSTA 180KM.

Port Augusta. Is that where I'm going? I don't remember deciding. But the car keeps moving forward, so I must have decided something.

More time passes. The darkness is absolute now, pressing in from all sides. The single headlight feels pathetically small against it. I could be the last person on earth. I could be driving through nothing, through nowhere, through a void.

Maybe I am.

Maybe I died back there at the cliff. Maybe this is what comes after, an endless drive through darkness, alone forever with what I've done.

The thought should terrify me, but I'm too numb to feel anything.

Another sign appears in the headlight: PORT AUGUSTA 95KM.

Closer. Whatever Port Augusta is, I'm getting closer to it.

My head nods forward. I jerk awake, the car swerving slightly. Adrenaline floods my system. I shake my head, trying to clear it, but that just makes everything blur more.

Blood and tears and dried sweat cake my face. I must look like a monster. Feel like one too.

Father's face keeps appearing in my mind. Not the face from the cliff, the angry, violent face, but an older memory. Father before the war. Father when Mother was still alive. Father lifting me onto his shoulders so I could see the fireworks. Father laughing. Father whole.

When did he break?

When did I?

The darkness outside seems to be pressing closer, seeping in through the broken windscreen. I can hear things in it, whispers, maybe, or just the wind. Or maybe the static finally breaking through, finding me even without the radio.

I press harder on the accelerator. The Volvo shudders but speeds up.

Another sign: PORT AUGUSTA 47KM.

I'm going to make it. Whatever happens after, at least I'll make it this far.

The sky ahead starts to lighten, not with dawn, but with something else. Artificial light. Civilisation. People.

People who will ask questions.

People who will want to know why I'm covered in blood, why the windscreen is cracked, why I'm alone.

People who will want to know where Father is.

Panic flutters in my chest, but I push it down. I'll figure it out. I always figure it out. I'll tell them... what? What will I tell them?

The truth? That Father tried to hurt me again and I defended myself?

But Father is dead. Has been dead for years, hasn't he? The doctors told me that. The staff at Greenplace told me that.

No. Wait. That's not right.

Father was just, he was right there, I killed him. Twice.

A wave of panic washes over me, how many times do I have to kill him? When will he stop?

My thoughts are tangling together, past and present bleeding into each other until I can't tell what's real and what's memory and what's something else entirely.

The lights of Port Augusta grow brighter. I can see the glow of it now, spreading across the horizon like a false dawn. Orange streetlights. Building lights. The lights of the living world that I'm about to drive into, covered in death.

One more sign: PORT AUGUSTA 12KM.

My hands are shaking on the wheel. The numbness is starting to crack, and underneath it is something terrible. Fear. Guilt. Horror. All of it waiting to break through.

But not yet. Not yet.

Just a little further.

The first buildings appear, industrial things, dark and hulking against the night sky. Then houses. Then streetlights, flooding the road with orange light that makes everything look unreal, washed out, like a photograph left too long in the sun.

I slow down. The Volvo rolls through empty streets. It must be very late, or very early. No one is around. All the windows are dark.

Good. That's good. Maybe I can just pass through. Maybe I can just...

Flashing lights in the rearview mirror.

Blue and red.

A siren, wailing like a wounded animal.

My heart stops.

Police.

The car behind me is a police car.

For a moment, I consider running. Just pressing the accelerator down and running until I can't run anymore.

But I'm so tired. So, so tired.

And maybe, maybe this is right. Maybe this is how it should end.

I pull over to the side of the road.

The police car pulls in behind me, lights still flashing, painting everything in alternating blue and red.

I sit there, hands on the wheel, dried blood cracking on my face, and wait.

A car door opens. Footsteps approach.

I reach under the driver's seat. My fingers find cold metal.

The knife. Father's knife. The one he always kept there, "for safety reasons," he'd say.

I pull it out. Hold it in my left hand. Fold my arm across my body so the blade is hidden below the door sill, my right hand free to wind the window down.

The footsteps get closer.

Knock, knock, knock.

I take a deep breath.

Wind down the window.

A policeman's face appears. Young. Concerned. Alive.

"Evening, miss," he says. "Are you alright? I noticed your headlight's out and your windscreen's damaged. Have you been in an accident?"

I open my mouth to answer.

But I don't know what to say.

I don't know how to explain any of this.

I don't know how to tell him that the past finally caught up with me, that I killed it, that I've been driving through the dark trying to outrun what I've done.

So I just sit there, the knife cold and heavy in my hidden hand, and stare at him.

Waiting for whatever comes next.

Chapter 10

Constable Peter Harris had been on the night shift for three years, and in that time, he'd seen plenty of strange things roll through Port Augusta at odd hours. Drunk miners. Runaway teenagers. The occasional tourist who'd taken a wrong turn somewhere around Ceduna and ended up hopelessly lost.

But the cream-coloured Volvo with the smashed headlight and spiderwebbed windscreen was something different.

He'd spotted it from two blocks away, the way it was moving, too slow and too careful, like the driver was either very drunk or very scared. When it passed under a streetlight, Peter had seen the damage to the front end and known immediately something was wrong.

He'd flicked on his lights and siren, expecting the car to pull over right away. Instead, it had kept going for another block, slow and steady, before finally easing to the curb.

That hesitation bothered him.

Peter radioed in his location, then grabbed his torch and stepped out of the patrol car. The street was empty; it was nearly three in the morning on a Sunday. Nothing was open. No witnesses if this went sideways.

His hand instinctively went to his hip, fingers brushing the handle of his baton. Not that he expected trouble. Just habit.

As he approached the driver's side, his torch beam swept across the damage. The windscreen was cracked in a starburst pattern, like something heavy had hit it. Something about the size and shape of a human body, his training whispered. The front left headlight was completely gone. Deep scratches in the paintwork.

This wasn't just a blown tire or a kangaroo strike. This was serious.

He reached the window and tapped on it with his knuckles. "Evening, miss. Are you alright? I noticed your headlight's out and your windscreen's damaged. Have you been in an accident?"

The window rolled down slowly.

And Peter's breath caught.

The girl, young woman, really, probably early twenties, was covered in blood. It was dried and cracking across her forehead, smeared down her face, matted in her hair. Her eyes were wide and unfocused, like she was looking at something far away. She wore an out-of-date red polka dot dress that would have been cheerful in any other circumstance but now looked macabre with the blood and the strange, vacant expression on her face.

"Miss?" Peter said again, his voice more urgent now. "Are you injured? Do you need an ambulance?"

She just stared at him. Not blank, exactly. There was something going on behind those eyes. But whatever it was, it wasn't quite connecting to the present moment.

"Miss, I need you to tell me what happened. Have you been in an accident?"

Still nothing.

Peter's instincts were screaming now. Something was very wrong here. The blood, the damage to the car, the girl's strange affect, none of it added up to anything good.

"I'm going to need you to step out of the vehicle," he said, keeping his voice calm and professional. "Just want to make sure you're not seriously hurt."

The girl's eyes finally focused on him. Really looked at him for the first time.

And Peter saw something in that look that made his blood run cold. Not fear. Not confusion. Something else. Something calculating.

"Miss?" he said, taking an involuntary step back.

Her right hand moved to open the door, and Peter relaxed slightly. Good. She was cooperating.

But as the door swung open and she started to step out, Peter saw the other hand. The left hand that had been hidden below the door frame.

She was holding a knife.

A large carving knife, the blade catching the orange glow of the streetlights.

"Whoa!" Peter's hand went to his baton, pulling it free. "Drop the knife! Drop it now!"

But the girl kept coming, stepping out of the car, the knife held loosely at her side. She wasn't threatening him with it, exactly. Wasn't raising it or making any aggressive moves.

But she wasn't dropping it either.

"Miss, I need you to put down the knife. Right now. Put it on the ground and step away from it."

She looked down at the knife in her hand, like she'd forgotten it was there. Then back up at Peter.

"He kept it under the seat," she said. Her voice was quiet, almost dreamy. "For safety reasons, he said."

"That's fine, that's okay," Peter said, trying to keep his voice steady. "But I need you to put it down now. Can you do that for me?"

"I don't feel safe without it."

"I understand. But you're safe now. I'm a police officer. I'm here to help you. But I can't help you if you're holding a weapon. Do you understand?"

She seemed to consider this. The knife wavered slightly in her grip.

"That's it," Peter encouraged. "Just set it down. Nice and slow."

For a moment, he thought she was going to comply. Her hand moved, lowering the knife toward the ground.

But then her eyes went distant again, looking past him at something only she could see.

"He's still there," she whispered. "I can see him. He's always there."

"Who's there, miss? Who are you talking about?"

"Father."

The word sent a chill down Peter's spine. The way she said it, flat, emotionless, like she was stating a fact about the weather.

"Where is your father, miss? Is he in the car?"

She shook her head slowly. "I left him. On the road. I had to. He was going to..." She stopped, swallowed hard. "I couldn't let him. Not again."

Christ. Peter's mind was racing through possibilities, each one worse than the last. Domestic violence? Had she been running from an abusive father? Had there been a confrontation?

Had she...?

No. Don't jump to conclusions. Get the knife first, then sort out the rest.

"Miss, I need you to tell me where your father is. Is he injured? Does he need help?"

"He's dead." She said it simply, matter-of-factly. "I killed him."

The words hung in the air between them.

Peter's hand tightened on his baton. "Miss, I need you to very carefully set down that knife and put your hands where I can see them."

But she wasn't listening anymore. Her eyes had gone completely vacant, staring through him at nothing.

"I kept my eyes on the road," she murmured. "Just like he taught me. Keep your eyes on the road, Mary. Don't look away. Keep driving."

"Mary? Is that your name? Mary, I'm going to need you to..."

She moved so fast Peter barely had time to react. Not toward him, she wasn't attacking. She was just moving, suddenly animated after all that stillness. The knife clattered to the ground as she stumbled forward, and Peter caught her just as her legs gave out.

She was saying something, over and over, but he couldn't make it out at first. Then he realised, she was counting.

"One, two, three. One, two, three. One, two, three."

"It's okay," Peter said, lowering her gently to sit on the curb. "It's going to be okay. I'm going to get you help."

He kicked the knife away, out of reach, then keyed his radio. "This is Harris. I need an ambulance at my location immediately. Female, early twenties, possible head injury, experiencing some kind of psychological episode. Also requesting backup and a supervisor. We may have a related incident somewhere on the highway, possible fatality. Over."

Static, then: "Copy that, Harris. Ambulance is en route. ETA five minutes."

Peter crouched down beside the girl, beside Mary. She'd stopped counting and was just sitting there now, staring at her hands.

"Mary? Can you hear me? Do you know where you are?"

"Port Augusta," she whispered.

"That's right. You're in Port Augusta. You're safe now. No one's going to hurt you."

She looked up at him, and for just a moment, her eyes cleared. Really focused. Really saw him.

"I couldn't let him hurt me again," she said. "I couldn't. Do you understand? I had to stop him."

"I understand," Peter said, even though he didn't. Not really. Not yet.

But he would. Once they found whatever she'd left behind on that dark highway, he would understand all too well.

In the distance, he could hear the wail of the ambulance siren, getting closer.

Mary heard it too. Her eyes went wide with panic.

"No," she said. "No, not the sirens. Please not the sirens."

"It's just an ambulance," Peter tried to reassure her. "They're coming to help you."

But she was shaking her head, hands over her ears, rocking back and forth.

"Make it stop. Make it stop. I can't think. I can't."

The ambulance pulled up, its lights painting the street in red and white. Mary screamed.

And Peter Harris, three years on the job and thinking he'd seen everything, realised he had absolutely no idea what he'd just stumbled into.

Chapter 11

The ambulance is too bright. Too white. Too loud with voices and beeping machines and the siren that won't stop won't stop won't stop.

"Mary, can you hear me? Can you tell me where you're hurt?"

A woman's face appears above me. Kind eyes. Concerned. But I don't trust kind eyes anymore. Kind eyes can lie.

"Where does it hurt, love?"

Everywhere. Nowhere. I don't know anymore.

Hands touching me. Gentle but insistent. Checking my head, my arms, shining a light in my eyes that makes me flinch away.

"Pupils are reactive but sluggish. Possible concussion. We need to get her to emergency."

The ambulance starts moving and my stomach lurches. I try to sit up but hands press me back down.

"It's okay, Mary. Just lie still. We're taking you to hospital. You're going to be fine."

The woman's trying to keep me calm, I can tell. Her voice is soft, soothing. She touches my shoulder gently.

"I like your dress, Mary," she says, casual, trying to distract me. "The polka dots are lovely."

I smile. Just for a second. Automatic. "Thank you, it's his favourite."

Then I go back to staring at nothing.

I see it though; the paramedic's eyes flick up. Meet Peter's eyes through the ambulance window. Something passes between them. A look. A knowing look.

They know something. They're talking about me without words.

My chest tightens. What do they know? What did I say? The paranoia crawls up my throat like bile.

Hospital. The word triggers something. A memory or a fear or both at once.

I don't want to go to the hospital. Bad things happen at hospitals. They keep you there. They make you take pills.

They turn on the radio and won't turn it off no matter how much you beg.

"No," I manage to say. "No hospital."

"You need medical attention, love. You've got a nasty cut on your head. We just need to make sure you're alright."

But I'm not alright. I'll never be alright again.

I close my eyes and try to disappear. Try to make myself so small that no one can see me. But the hands keep touching, keep checking, keep asking questions I don't know how to answer.

"What's your full name, Mary?"

Mary... what? Do I have a last name? I must have. Everyone has a last name.

"Where do you live?"

Greenplace. By the river. But that's not right, is it? Or is it?

"Is there someone we can call? Family? Friends?"

Father is dead. Mother is dead. There's no one left.

The ambulance stops. Doors open. Cold air rushes in. I'm being moved, lifted, rolled. Fluorescent lights pass overhead like a strobe. More voices. More questions.

"Female, approximately twenty-three years old, head injury, possible assault victim. She's been saying she killed her father."

The words fade in and out like a bad radio signal. I float somewhere above my body, watching it all happen to someone else. That girl on the gurney with the blood-matted hair and the polka dot dress. That's not me. That can't be me.

A face appears above me again. Different person. Male. White coat.

"Mary? I'm Dr. Johnstone. You're at Port Augusta Hospital. We're going to take care of you, but I need to ask you some questions. Can you tell me what happened tonight?"

What happened? What happened?

I drove. I ran. I killed Father. No, Father was already dead. David. His name was David. Wasn't it?

The memories are sliding away from me like water, impossible to hold.

"I don't remember," I whisper.

Peter Harris stood by the Volvo as the ambulance pulled away, its siren fading into the early morning quiet. The knife lay on the ground where he'd kicked it, the blade dull in the streetlight.

He called in to the station again. "This is Harris. The girl is en route to hospital. She's been making statements about killing her father. Given the condition of the vehicle and her claims, I'm requesting immediate dispatch of detectives and crime scene investigators. We need to search the highway for possible victims."

"Copy that. How far back are we talking?"

Peter looked at the Volvo again, the damage, the blood. "She came from the west. Could be anywhere along the Nullarbor. She mentioned leaving him 'on the road.' No specifics."

"Jesus. Alright, we'll coordinate with Ceduna and Penong stations, see if they've had any reports. Stay with the vehicle until forensics arrives."

"Will do."

Peter hung up and approached the car more carefully now. He pulled out his torch and swept it across the interior. Blood on the steering wheel. Blood on the driver's seat. More blood dried on the dashboard. The passenger seat was relatively clean, but there were impressions there, someone had been sitting there recently.

The back seat had a dark green duffle bag.

Peter photographed everything with his personal camera, he'd learned the hard way that the official photographers sometimes took hours to arrive. Then he carefully opened the back door and examined the bag without touching it.

Military-style. American, by the look of it.

There was a name tag sewn onto the side: SGT. J. COLEMAN.

Peter's stomach dropped.

The girl had said "father." But this bag belonged to someone else. Possibly someone who'd been in the car with her.

He keyed his radio again. "We may have multiple victims. I've found evidence of at possibly one other person in the vehicle. Military identification. Stand by for details."

As he waited for backup, Peter walked a slow circle around the Volvo, documenting everything. The front left side had taken the most damage, the headlight smashed, deep dents in the bonnet, scratches that looked like they could have been made by... clothing? Buttons?

Like someone had rolled across it.

His torch beam caught something on the roof. He moved closer.

Hair. Human hair, caught in a dent near the back of the roof.

Peter's hands were shaking slightly as he photographed it. Whatever had happened out there on the Nullarbor, it was bad. Really bad.

Another patrol car pulled up, followed by a forensics van. Peter briefed them quickly, showed them what he'd found.

"We need to trace her route," Detective Morrison said, a heavy-set man in his fifties who Peter had worked with before. "Find out where she stopped, what happened. This much blood, this much damage, someone's dead out there."

"She kept saying 'I killed him,'" Peter offered. "Said she couldn't let him hurt her again. Something about keeping her eyes on the road."

Morrison nodded grimly. "Domestic situation gone bad. Father-daughter. We've seen it before. But usually they call it in, they don't drive three hundred kilometres covered in blood."

"There's something else, sir. The girl, Mary, she wasn't quite... present. Dissociated. Like she wasn't entirely sure what was real."

"Shock will do that."

"Maybe. But this seemed like something more."

Morrison looked at him. "What are you thinking?"

Peter hesitated. "I think we need to check if she's got a history. The way she was acting, the things she was saying, it wasn't just shock. It was like she was living in two different realities at once."

"We'll run her through the system. In the meantime, let's get this car processed and get units out on the highway.

First light, we start searching."

I wake up in a white room. Clean sheets. Soft pillow. Bandage on my head.

For a moment, I don't remember where I am or how I got here.

Then it comes back in fragments. The ambulance. The hospital. The questions I couldn't answer.

I try to sit up but my head spins. A hand presses gently on my shoulder.

"Easy now. You've had quite a night."

A nurse. Middle-aged woman with kind eyes and tired smile. She's wearing pale blue scrubs and has a clipboard tucked under her arm.

"Where am I?" My voice is hoarse.

"Port Augusta Hospital. You were brought in a few hours ago. Don't you remember?"

Hours ago. What time is it now? How long have I been here?

"What's your name?" the nurse asks.

"Mary."

"Mary what?"

I open my mouth but nothing comes out. What is my last name? I should know this. Why don't I know this?

"That's alright. We'll figure it out. The police will be wanting to talk to you when you're feeling better."

Police. The word sends ice through my veins.

"There was a policeman," I say slowly. "On the road. I had a knife."

"Yes. Constable Harris. He's the one who called the ambulance. He's very concerned about you." She pauses.

"He said you told him you'd killed someone. Your father."

Father.

The memories rush back. The cliff. The eyes. The hands. The fight. The car. The body in the road.

"I did," I whisper. "I did kill him."

The nurse's expression doesn't change. "The police are trying to locate him now. They need you to tell them where he is."

"On the road. The Nullarbor. I left him there."

She writes something on her clipboard. "Can you tell me what happened? Why you were out there?"

I try to put it together, try to make it make sense. But the pieces don't fit. The memories contradict each other.

Was I with Father? Or was I with David? Was James real? Did any of it happen?

"I don't know," I finally say. "I can't remember."

"That's alright, love. The doctor thinks you might have a concussion. Memory loss is normal with head injuries. It might come back to you."

But I don't want it to come back. I want to forget all of it. Want to erase the past twenty-four hours—or is it forty-eight? How long have I been driving?

"What day is it?" I ask.

"Sunday morning. The nineteenth of November."

The nineteenth. I left... when did I leave? Friday? Saturday? Time has lost all meaning.

The nurse checks my vital signs, writes more notes. "You just rest now. The police will want to talk to you later, but for now, you need to recover. You're safe here. Nobody's going to hurt you."

Safe. The word sounds foreign. Impossible.

How can I be safe when the danger is inside my own head?

She leaves, closing the door softly behind her. I'm alone in the white room with my fractured memories and the terrible certainty of what I've done.

I killed Father.

Or did I kill David?

Or are they the same person?

I close my eyes and try to remember, but all I see is blood and broken glass and the endless red road stretching out ahead of me.

Always driving. Always running. Never quite escaping.

Chapter 12

Detective Morrison's phone rang at 6:47 AM, just as the sun was breaking over Port Augusta.

"Morrison."

"Sir, it's Constable Davies from Ceduna. We've got a body. Male, on the Eyre Highway about three hundred kilometres west of your position. Road train driver called it in about twenty minutes ago. Says it's been there a while."

Morrison was already reaching for his jacket. "Description?"

"White male, thirties, long hair. Significant trauma consistent with a vehicle strike. And sir—there's a detail you should know. The body is lying in the middle of fresh tire tracks leading off the highway. Volvo treads, by the look of them."

"We're on our way. Secure the scene. Nobody touches anything until we arrive."

Morrison grabbed Peter Harris and they drove west, away from the rising sun. The radio crackled with updates—more units being dispatched, the medical examiner en route from Ceduna.

Three hundred kilometres. Mary had driven through the night, alone, with a dead man in her rearview mirror. Had she looked back? Had she known he was dead?

The drive took them nearly four hours, the empty highway stretching endlessly ahead.

They reached the scene just after eleven AM. Two patrol cars had blocked off the highway, orange cones forcing traffic to slow. A massive road train was parked on the shoulder, its driver sitting in the shade, waiting.

The body lay about five meters off the road, partially hidden by a slight rise in the ground. That's why earlier traffic had missed it, the predawn darkness, the body just far enough from the highway to be out of the headlight sweep.

Morrison and Peter approached carefully, following the marked path the first responders had laid out.

The man lay face-down in the red dust, one arm bent at an impossible angle. Blood had pooled beneath him and dried black in the dirt. His clothes, the mustard turtleneck, the bell-bottom trousers, were torn and filthy.

"Help me turn him," Morrison said to the medical examiner who'd arrived just before them.

They rolled the body carefully onto its back. The face was swollen and discoloured, nose clearly broken, but the features were still recognisable enough for identification.

Peter pulled out his camera and photographed the body from multiple angles while Morrison searched the pockets.

"Wallet," Morrison said, flipping it open. "David Robert Morrison. Age thirty-three. Perth address." He looked up at Peter. "Same surname as me. No relation, obviously, but still feels strange."

"What else?"

Morrison laid out the contents. "Driver's license. Bank cards. Receipt from a motel in Norseman dated three days ago." He paused, studying the receipt. "Paid cash. No name except his on the receipt."

Peter crouched down, examining the ground around the body. "Look at this. You can see where the car came from, straight line off the highway. And here..." he pointed "these marks. The body rolled. From the impact, then off the back of the vehicle."

"Matches the damage pattern we saw on the Volvo," Morrison agreed. "He was hit from the front, went up onto the bonnet, over the roof, off the back. Died on impact, probably. Massive head trauma."

The medical examiner was examining the body more closely. "Contusions on his lower abdomen and groin area. Pre-mortem. Happened shortly before death."

"Someone hit him?" Peter asked.

"Or kicked him. Hard enough to bruise significantly."

Morrison stood, looking back toward the highway, then at the long stretch of empty road leading west. "So, our girl is with this man, David. They're traveling together. Something happens. She kicks him in the groin, runs to the car, and runs him down as he's chasing her. Then drives three hundred kilometres to Port Augusta in a state of complete psychological breakdown."

"She said she killed her father," Peter reminded him.

"But this isn't her father. He's too young. Unless..." Morrison paused. "We need to find out who Mary actually is. Run her description through missing persons. Contact hospitals. A young woman who thinks her traveling companion is her father. That's not just trauma. That's something deeper."

"Which hospitals?"

Morrison looked up to Peter, then up to the sky. Birds were circling high above, waiting to feast on the fresh flesh. He glanced back to Peter and shrugged. "All of them."

Another constable jogged over. "Sir, we've got reports of a vehicle matching the Volvo's description at the Nullarbor Roadhouse two days ago, around two PM. The attendant remembers a young woman in a polka dot dress with a man, sounds like our victim here. Said the girl seemed agitated."

"Just the two of them?" Morrison asked.

"That's what she said. The man and the girl."

Morrison thought about the military duffle bag in the back of the Volvo. "So where did the bag come from? Maybe they picked up a hitchhiker after the roadhouse. Or maybe..." He paused. "Maybe Mary stole it from somewhere. That could have started an argument with David. He finds out she's stolen from someone, confronts her about it."

Peter nodded. "And it escalates from there."

The medical examiner worked on processing David's body. Morrison and Peter stepped back, scanning the ground around the scene.

"Look, over there," Peter said, walking across the road. "Footprints in the dust. Multiple sets." He bent down to take a look. "All boot prints."

Morrison joined him. The tracks were clear in the red dust, several sets of boots, overlapping and confused.

"They walked here from that direction," Peter pointed south from the highway. "On foot."

"Let's follow the trail."

They walked carefully, preserving the footprints. The tracks led them towards the coast, across the scrubland. After about three minutes, they could hear it—the ocean.

Ahead, the land dropped away. The cliff edge.

The footprints led straight toward it, a chaotic mess of prints, some overlapping, but clearly three distinct sets going forward.

"Three sets going to the cliff," Peter said, crouching down to examine them carefully. "But coming back—only two sets. The heaviest prints stop at the edge."

Morrison approached the cliff carefully. The footprints were everywhere here, a confusion of tracks in the churned-up dirt. Clear signs of a struggle. Feet sliding. Bodies pushing.

Peter was at the cliff edge now, looking down. Then he stopped, tilting his head. "Sir. Do you hear that?"

Morrison joined him. Below, the ocean crashed against the rocks. But over that sound, something else. A harsh, repetitive calling. He looked up. Seabirds. Dozens of them, wheeling and diving in a tight circle about thirty meters down the cliff face.

"They're circling something," Peter said quietly.

Morrison's stomach tightened. He moved to the edge and looked down.

The cliff wasn't completely vertical; it stepped down in rocky shelves before ending at the ocean. On one of those shelves, perhaps a third of the way down, something dark lay sprawled across the stone.

The birds were taking turns landing near it, hopping closer, then flying away.

"Christ," Morrison breathed. "There's someone down there."

Peter was already on the radio, calling for a rescue team. Morrison kept his eyes on the body below. Dark clothing. Dark hair. Completely still.

"Second victim," he said quietly. "Has to be. James Coleman."

"How do we get down there?"

"We don't. We wait for the rescue squad with proper equipment." Morrison backed away from the edge, his mind racing. "So, they came out here, all three of them. To look at the ocean, maybe. There's a struggle at the cliff edge. Coleman goes over. Falls onto that shelf. Dead or dying."

"Then what?"

"Then David confronts Mary. Maybe he's horrified, maybe he's trying to help. Either way, she panics. They struggle, she kicks him, runs. He chases her back to the highway where the car is. That's when she runs him over. Then drives east until she can't drive anymore."

Peter looked at the disturbed earth, the footprints, the cliff edge. "Self-defence?"

"Maybe. Or maybe she pushed Coleman off that cliff deliberately and killed David to cover it up." Morrison ran a hand over his face. "Either way, two men are dead, and we've got a young woman who can't tell us what's real and what isn't."

The rescue team arrived from Ceduna four hours later, just after three PM. It took them another two hours to set up the rappelling equipment and carefully descend the cliff face to reach the body.

Morrison and Peter watched from above as the team worked. The body was secured, carefully lifted, and slowly brought up the cliff in a rescue basket. When they finally laid it on the ground at the clifftop, Morrison could see why the birds had been circling.

The body had been there for at least twenty-four hours in the heat. The face was swollen, discoloured. But worse was the trauma, the skull clearly fractured, one arm twisted at an impossible angle, the dark green jacket torn and stained with blood and seawater spray.

The medical examiner examined the body carefully. "Massive blunt force trauma consistent with a fall from height. Multiple fractures. He likely died on impact."

Morrison searched for identification, already knowing what he'd find. The dog tags around the corpse's neck confirmed it: SGT. JAMES COLEMAN, U.S. ARMY.

"American soldier," Morrison said. "Hitchhiker, probably. Picked up somewhere along the highway." He looked at the cliff edge, then back toward where the highway lay. "He comes out here with them to look at the view. Or someone calls him over. Either way, there's a struggle, and he goes over the edge."

"Then David and Mary have their confrontation," Peter continued. "And she kills him too."

Morrison stood, looking out at the endless ocean. Two men dead. A young woman who thought she'd killed her father. And no clear answers about what had really happened in this remote spot.

"We need to find out who she really is," Morrison said. "Because until we know that we can't know why she thinks David Morrison was her father. Or what made her kill him."

He took one last look at the cliff edge, at the rocks below, at the seabirds that had led them to James Coleman's body.

Three people had come to this beautiful, terrible place. Only one had left.

And she'd been covered in blood, clutching a knife, counting to three.

The investigation was just beginning.

Chapter 13

I wake up slowly, swimming up through layers of fog. The bed is soft. Clean white sheets. Sunlight streaming through a window.

For a moment, everything is perfect.

I'm in a hotel. No, a hospital? But not like the one I've been in before. This is nice. Quiet. Safe.

David must have brought me here. We're in Adelaide. We made it.

I stretch, feeling the pull of bandages on my head. I must have hurt myself somehow. Hit my head? The details are fuzzy, but it doesn't matter. We're here. We're safe. We can start our new life.

A nurse comes in, different from the others. Younger. She smiles when she sees I'm awake.

"Good morning, Mary. How are you feeling?"

"Good," I say, smiling back. "Is David here? When can I see him?"

Her smile falters. "Just rest for now, love. The police want to talk to you. Are you up for that?"

Police? Why would the police want to talk to me?

"I don't understand," I say.

"They'll explain everything. Let me go get them."

She leaves and I sit up, confused. The room is bright and clean. There's a window and a couple of chairs. Normal. Everything seems so normal.

***

Outside in the hallway, Detective Morrison and Peter Harris stood reviewing their notes.

"The sedation should be wearing off by now," the doctor had told them. "But I need to warn you, her mental state is extremely fragile. She has periods of clarity followed by complete dissociation. She doesn't seem to understand that the men are dead."

"We need to know who she is," Morrison said. "We've run her description through every database we have. Nothing. No missing persons reports matching her. No identification except a first name."

"The clothing is the key," Peter suggested. "Those sixties-style clothes. She's been isolated, living in the past."

"Or she did it to herself," Morrison countered. "Trauma can make people retreat to safer times."

The nurse appeared. "She's awake. And she's asking for David."

Morrison and Peter exchanged glances. "She doesn't know," Peter said quietly.

They entered the room. Mary was sitting up in bed, looking small and lost in a hospital gown. Her head was bandaged, her face still showing traces of dried blood despite cleaning. But her expression was bright, almost cheerful.

"Hello," she said. "Are you the police? The nurse said you wanted to talk to me. Is this about the car? I know I was driving without a license, but David was teaching me. He said it would be okay."

***

Inside the room, I watch the two men enter.

"Can I sit by the window?" I ask. The bed feels too confining, too much like being trapped.

One of the men nods. "Of course."

I get up slowly, my legs shaky, and move to the chair by the window. Outside, I can see the estuary spreading out below, water and land meeting, birds wheeling over the mudflats. It's beautiful. Open. Safe.

One of them pulls up a chair beside me. "Mary, I'm Detective Morrison. This is Constable Harris. We need to ask you some questions about what happened."

I keep my eyes on the view outside. The water. The land. Real things. Solid things.

"What happened?" I say, genuinely confused. "We drove to Adelaide. Or... are we in Adelaide? I thought we were almost there. David has a job here. Engineering. At the Space Agency."

"Mary," Morrison says gently. "Do you remember stopping on the highway? Near a cliff?"

My eyes drift up from the estuary, searching the sky. Where are the birds? They were just there. Where did they go?

"I don't... there was someone. A man. James? No, that's not right. Or is it?" My hands grip the arms of the chair. I need to see a bird. Need to see something flying. Free.

"Where's David? He'll explain. He always explains things when I get confused."

Peter leaned forward. "Mary, David can't explain. David is dead."

The room tilts. The white walls start closing in. My eyes scan the sky frantically. No birds. Why aren't there any birds?

"No," I whisper. "No, that didn't happen. You're confused. You're thinking of someone else."

My breathing is getting faster. The sky is empty. Too empty. I need to see...

There. A gull. White wings against blue. I watch it, following its path, and my breathing slows.

The detective, Morrison, he has kind eyes, but his voice is firm. "Mary, David Robert Morrison is dead. We found his body on the Eyre Highway. He was struck by a vehicle. Your vehicle."

"No," I whisper. "No, that didn't happen. You're confused. You're thinking of someone else."

"We also found another man," Morrison continues. "An American soldier named James Coleman. He died at the bottom of a cliff. Were you there when it happened?"

James. The name triggers something. Eyes in the mirror. Watching eyes. Father's eyes.

"I don't... I can't..."

"Mary, we need to know what happened. Did you push James Coleman off that cliff?"

"I don't know!" My voice is rising, panic clawing up my throat. "I don't remember! I was at the ocean and then, and then..."

"And then what?"

And then Father was there. Father with his hands and his eyes and his voice saying come here baby you know you like it.

"It was him," I hear myself say. "It was Father. He tried to hurt me again."

***

From his position beside her chair, Morrison sat back, watching the transformation happen in real time. Mary's face had changed, the cheerful confusion replaced by something harder, darker.

"Father?" he asked carefully. "Mary, your father wasn't there. It was David Morrison and James Coleman. Do you understand? David and James."

"No." She shook her head violently, her eyes leaving the estuary view to scan the empty sky above. "It was Father. He found me. He always finds me. No matter where I go, he finds me."

Morrison glanced at Peter. Had she noticed? The way her gaze changed depending on her mental state. When she was coherent, she looked down at the landscape, grounded. But when the confusion took over, her eyes went up, searching the sky like she was looking for an escape route.

"Mary, your father, where..."

"He deserved it!" she shouted suddenly, her voice raw. "He deserved what happened to him! Every time! Every single time he came to my room, every time he put his hands on me, every time he..." She stopped, breathing hard. "He deserved it."

Peter and Morrison exchanged glances. Every time. What did that mean?

"Mary," Morrison said slowly, "when you say 'every time,' what do you mean? How many times has this happened?"

But she wasn't listening anymore. Her eyes had gone distant again, staring at something beyond the walls. Up. Always up. Searching the empty sky.

"He keeps coming back," she whispered. "I kill him but he keeps coming back. In the car. In the mirror. In the man with the dark hair and the eyes that watch. He's always there. He'll always be there."

***

I'm barely aware of the detectives anymore.

Where are the birds? Why can't I see any birds? My chest tightens. The sky is too big, too empty, too...

There. Two cockatoos, their white feathers bright against the blue. I watch them circle and land in a tree. My breathing steadies.

Morrison and Peter exchanged a glance. Peter raised his eyebrows slightly, nodding toward Mary's changing focus, sky to land to sky again, tracking with her lucidity.

They think I'm crazy. I can see it in their faces. The way they look at each other. The way Morrison writes things down in his little notebook.

But I'm not crazy. I know what happened.

Father came back. He always comes back. Even though I killed him. Even though he's supposed to be dead.

He was in James. I saw it. Those eyes. Father's eyes.

And then he was in David. When David grabbed me, when he pushed me down, when he...

No. Wait.

Was that David? Or was that Father?

The memories are sliding around, refusing to stay still. I see David's face but it morphs into Father's face. I hear David's voice but it's Father's voice underneath.

Which one was real?

Which one did I kill?

"Mary," the detective is saying, "we need to know your full name. Your last name. Where you're from. Who your family is."

Family. The word is meaningless.

"Greenplace," I say. "I'm from Greenplace. By the river."

"Greenplace? Is that a street? A suburb?"

"It's home." But even as I say it, I'm not sure anymore. Is it home? Or is it something else?

The room is spinning again. The detective's face blurs into Father's face blurs into David's face.

My eyes dart upward. Where are they? Where did the birds go? I need to see them. Need to know they're still there.

The sky is empty again. Panic rises in my throat.

"He deserved it," I whisper, my voice tight. "Every time. He deserved it every time."

No birds. No birds anywhere. I can't breathe. Can't.

A magpie swoops past the window. Black and white. Free. Flying.

I let out a breath I didn't know I was holding.

***

In the corner of the room, Morrison stood and gestured for Peter to join him, speaking quietly while Mary remained fixated on the window.

"You see that?" Peter murmured. "The way she looks out the window?"

"I noticed," Morrison said. "When she's making sense, she looks down. At the estuary, the land. But when she loses it, she looks up. At the sky."

"And did you see when she started panicking? When there weren't any birds visible. She calmed down the second one appeared."

Morrison glanced back at Mary, who was now staring peacefully at the magpie on the window ledge, her expression almost serene. "She's looking for an escape. Something to follow. The birds represent freedom to her."

"Or she's looking for something," Peter suggested. "Something she can't find down here. On the ground. In reality."

"She's not making sense. One minute she's talking about David like he's alive, the next she's saying she killed her father. And this 'every time' business?"

"You think she's done this before?" Peter asked.

"I think she believes she has. Whether it actually happened..." Morrison shook his head. "We need to find out who she really is. This 'Greenplace' she mentioned, run it. Every database. Property records, business names, anything."

Peter nodded and slipped out of the room.

Morrison turned back to Mary. She was staring at the window now, her gaze fixed on the estuary below. Grounded. Present. At least for the moment.

"Mary, I want to help you. But I need you to help me understand. Who is your father? What's his name?"

"Dead," she said simply, her eyes on the mudflats. "He's dead. I made sure of it."

"When did he die?"

"Yesterday. On the road. I hit him with the car." She looked at Morrison, then back to the window. Her eyes drifted up to the sky. "Or was it years ago? I can't remember. Time doesn't work right anymore."

***

Alone with my thoughts, I lose myself in the emptiness above.

The sky is so big. So empty. Where are the birds?

"Mary?"

"He taught me to drive, you know," I continue, my voice dreamy now, eyes scanning the endless blue above. "Let me sit on his lap. Keep your eyes on the road, Mary. His hand going down, down... Keep your eyes on the road. Don't look. If you don't look, it's not happening."

***

Listening to her words, Morrison felt sick. "Mary, did your father abuse you?"

She laughed, a sound with no humour in it. "Abuse? Is that what you call it? He called it love. Special love for his special girl."

"When did this happen? How old were you?"

"Eight. Ten. Twelve. Fourteen. Every night the door would open. Every night until..." She stopped. "Until I made it stop."

"How did you make it stop?"

She looked at him then, really looked at him, and her eyes were completely clear. Completely sane. Focused on his face, then down to the estuary beyond, grounded in the present moment.

"I killed him," she said. "Just like I killed him yesterday. Just like I'll kill him tomorrow if he comes back again."

Morrison's blood ran cold. "Mary, who did you kill yesterday? Was it David Morrison? Or was it someone else in your mind?"

But she'd gone distant again, her moment of clarity passing like a cloud across the sun. Her gaze drifted upward, searching.

"The bird," she murmured, looking at the window. "Look at the bird. It can fly away. That's what I want to do. Fly away where he can't follow."

Morrison looked where she was pointing. A magpie sat on the window ledge, preening its feathers.

When he looked back, Mary was crying silently, tears running down her face.

"I just wanted to be free," she whispered. "Is that so wrong? To want to be free?"

***

Sitting here by the window, I don't know how long I cry. The detective doesn't try to stop me. He just waits.

Eventually, the tears run out. I feel empty. Hollow.

"What happens now?" I ask.

"Now we try to figure out who you are," Morrison says. "And what really happened out there on the Nullarbor."

"What if I don't know?" I say honestly. "What if I can't tell you because I don't know myself?"

"Then we'll find another way," he says.

But I can see in his eyes that he's not sure. Not sure of anything.

And neither am I.

All I know is that Father is dead. David is dead. James and Tommy are dead.

Tommy? Why does that name ring a bell?

And I'm still here, still breathing, still trapped inside my own head with memories that don't make sense and a past that won't stay in the past.

The bird flies away from the window.

I watch it go and wish I could follow.

Chapter 14

Peter Harris returned to Morrison's temporary office at Port Augusta station with a folder of papers. His expression was troubled.

"Found it," he said, dropping the folder on the desk. "Greenplace."

Morrison looked up from his notes. "What is it?"

"It's not a house or a suburb." Peter pulled out a document. "Greenplace Hospital for the Mentally Ill. Mosman Park, Perth. Psychiatric facility, been operating since the 1950s."

Morrison sat back slowly. "A psychiatric hospital."

"Mary Elizabeth Patterson. Age twenty-four. Patient at Greenplace on and off for the past ten years." Peter consulted his notes. "That's all they'd give me over the phone. Said they need official requests for full medical records."

"Ten years," Morrison said quietly. "Since she was fourteen."

"The administrator I spoke with confirmed she was on a supervised weekend release. Due back Monday morning. She's now officially listed as missing, along with her supervisor."

"David Morrison."

"Right. They said he was authorized to take her on a therapeutic outing. Wouldn't give me details about their relationship or why he was approved as her supervisor."

Morrison stood and walked to the window. "So Mary wasn't from a wealthy family with staff. She was a patient. The 'home' she talked about, Greenplace, was the institution."

"It was home to her. And David wasn't just some guy giving her a ride to start a new life. He was supposed to bring her back."

"But he didn't plan to, did he?" Morrison turned back. "She kept talking about moving to Adelaide. Starting fresh. David's job at the Space Agency. That wasn't the plan for a weekend release."

"So what was it? Was he helping her escape? Or was he..." Peter stopped.

"Taking advantage of a vulnerable patient?" Morrison finished. "That's what we need to find out. And we're not going to get those answers over the phone."

Peter nodded. "I was thinking the same thing. We need to go there. Talk to the staff who knew them both. See Mary's records. Understand what we're really dealing with here."

Morrison looked at the map on the wall. Perth to Port Augusta, nearly three thousand kilometres. "It's a long drive."

"We could fly, but?"

"But Mary came by car. If we're retracing what happened, we should follow her route." Morrison made a decision. "We'll drive. Stop at the motel in Norseman, the roadhouse, the cliff area. See if we can piece together the timeline properly."

"What about Mary?"

"We'll transport her back with us. Ambulance escort. The hospital wants her back, and she needs to be in proper care, not a general hospital ward." Morrison picked up the phone. "I'll arrange it. We leave tomorrow morning."

***

The next morning, Morrison and Peter met at the hospital. Mary was being prepared for transport, sedated, restrained for her own safety and others'. She looked small and fragile on the ambulance stretcher, her head still bandaged, wearing a hospital gown.

"She's been asking for David again," the nurse told them. "Doesn't remember we told her he's dead. The psychiatrist said the trauma is causing selective memory loss."

Morrison looked down at Mary. Her eyes were closed, but her hands were twitching slightly. He guessed she was dreaming of flying.

"Let's get her home," he said quietly.

The convoy left Port Augusta at dawn, Morrison and Peter in the lead car, the ambulance behind them, a local patrol car bringing up the rear for the first hundred kilometres. They drove in silence, watching the sun climb over the endless Nullarbor.

After a few hours, Morrison pulled over at the spot where they'd found David's body. The scene had been cleared, but the marks were still there, tire tracks, disturbed earth, a dark stain where blood had pooled.

"This is where it ended for him," Peter said.

Morrison looked back at the ambulance. Mary was inside, sedated, unaware they were standing at the place where she'd killed David. Or where she'd killed her father, in her mind.

They continued south, following the footprints they'd traced days before. The cliff was still there; yellow police tape fluttering in the wind. The ocean crashed against the rocks below where James Coleman had died.

"Two men dead in this one spot," Peter observed. "And Mary might not even remember it happening."

They drove on. Hours passed. The landscape blurred together, red earth, blue sky, endless nothing.

Eventually Morrison spotted the dirt track that led to a clearing where the Ceduna police had found evidence of camping.

"Should we check it?" Peter asked.

Morrison considered. "Might as well. See if they missed anything."

They followed the track to the open area. The flattened grass where a blanket had been. The tire impressions. It looked the same as the photographs they'd been sent, but now Morrison could picture it differently, David and Mary here, under the stars, David telling her about space and infinity and fresh starts. Mary feeling safe for maybe the first time in years.

And then the next morning, everything falling apart.

"They were happy here," Morrison said. "For one night, before it all went wrong. Looks like only the two of them stayed here. James Coleman must have been picked up between here and the cliffs."

"Things went south, quickly. No one could have known."

"Mary might have..."

Peter looked at Morrison, then kicked at the dirt. "If Coleman hadn't been picked up. If they'd just kept driving to Adelaide. Would it have ended differently?"

"We'll never know."

They returned to the convoy.

Late afternoon, they reached the roadhouse. Morrison pulled in, and Peter went inside while he stretched his legs.

The woman behind the counter recognized Peter immediately. "You're the police who were asking about that girl. Did you find her?"

"We did. She's with us now. Being transported back to Perth."

The woman's expression softened. "Poor thing. She looked so confused when she was here. Like a lost child. And that man with her, he seemed like he was trying to help, but..." she paused. "I've been thinking about it. The way he looked at her. Protective, yes. But also... possessive. Like she belonged to him."

Peter wrote that down. "Did they say anything to each other? Anything that stood out?"

"He kept telling her everything was going to be okay. That they'd be in Adelaide soon. That they could start fresh. They purchased sandwiches and drinks, nothing unusual." The woman shook her head. "But she kept looking at that newspaper date like she'd lost years, somewhere."

"She had," Peter said quietly. "Thank you."

They continued west as evening approached. The sun was setting now, painting the sky orange and purple. They'd need to stop for the night soon.

Morrison radioed the ambulance. "How's our passenger?"

"Sleeping. Vitals stable. But she's been talking in her sleep. Keeps saying 'keep your eyes on the road.'"

Morrison and Peter exchanged a glance.

"Her father taught her to drive," Peter said quietly. "While he was abusing her."

"If! If he was abusing her," replied Morrison. "This may all be in her head."

They drove until dark, then stopped at a motel in Ceduna. Mary was transferred to a secure room with medical supervision. Morrison and Peter took rooms on either side.

Peter couldn't sleep. He kept thinking about Mary in that room, sedated and dreaming, trapped in memories that wouldn't let her go. Kept thinking about David Morrison, was he a helper or predator? Victim or accomplice?

And he kept thinking about the knife. The knife she'd carried but never used. Insurance against a father who kept coming back. What if she saw her father in *him* when he pulled her over? He shuddered with the thought. Would he be another victim or would he have actually used his batten to stop a young delusional girl?

The next morning, they continued west. Norseman appeared on the horizon, the motel where Mary had disappeared in the night, where David had woken to find her gone, where everything had started to unravel.

Morrison pulled into the motel parking lot. Same cheap building, same dusty lot. Different ending.

The manager remembered them. "You found her, then? The girl? I read she was missing in last night's paper."

"We found her. She's being taken back to Perth."

"And the man? David Morrison?"

"Dead. Killed during an incident."

The manager shook his head. "He seemed like a nice fellow when they checked in. Paid cash, said they were heading to Adelaide. Asked for one room." He paused. "But there was something odd. When they were filling out the paperwork, the girl, Mary, she asked me if there was a park nearby. A park where she could play. I thought it was strange, her being in her twenties and all, asking about a playground like a little kid. I looked at David, wondering what that was about, and he just laughed it off. Said she was young at heart."

Morrison and Peter exchanged glances.

"Young at heart," Peter repeated quietly.

"Yeah. But it wasn't that, was it?" The manager's expression darkened. "Something was wrong with her. The way she talked, the way she looked around like everything was new and scary. I should have said something. Should have asked more questions."

"You couldn't have known," Morrison said, though he wasn't sure that was true.

"Seemed like a couple. But now you're telling me she was a patient and he was, what? Kidnapping her?"

"We don't know yet," Morrison admitted. "That's what we're going to Perth to find out."

They drove the final stretch into Perth, arriving at sunset. The city sprawled before them, civilisation after days of empty desert.

And there, in Mosman Park, by the river, was Greenplace.

It didn't look like a prison. It looked almost pleasant, manicured lawns, trees, a large building that could have been a school or hospital from the outside. But Morrison could see the high fence, the secure entrance, the barred windows on the upper floors.

This was where Mary had spent nearly half of her life. In and out, the records had said. What did that mean? Released and readmitted? Escaping and being brought back?

They pulled up to the entrance. The ambulance behind them. The local patrol car had peeled off at the city limits.

A woman in nurse's scrubs was waiting at the entrance, older, tired eyes, but a kind face.

"Detective Morrison?" she called. "I'm Nurse Gladys. We've been expecting you."

Morrison and Peter got out. Behind them, the ambulance doors opened and Mary was being unloaded on the stretcher, still sedated.

Nurse Gladys's expression crumpled when she saw her. "Oh, Mary. Poor love. What happened to you out there?"

"That's what we're here to find out," Morrison said. "We need to know everything. About Mary. About David Morrison. About what was really going on."

Nurse Gladys looked at him, and in her eyes Morrison saw something he hadn't expected.

Guilt.

"Come inside," she said quietly. "There's a lot you need to know. And I'm not sure all of it will make you feel better about what happened."

As they wheeled Mary inside, Morrison heard it, the radio. Constant, pervasive, filling the halls with voices and music and static.

Mary stirred on the stretcher, her hands trying to cover her ears, even in her sedated state, a small sound of distress escaping her lips.

"The radio," Morrison said. "She hates the radio."

"I know," Nurse Gladys said, her voice heavy with something that might have been regret. "We all know."

And Morrison realised there was far more to this story than anyone had told them yet.

Chapter 15

Nurse Gladys led Morrison and Peter through the corridors of Greenplace. The radio followed them, a constant drone of music and voices that seemed to seep from the walls themselves. Morrison could hear it coming from every room they passed, patients sitting or lying in beds, staring at nothing, the radio playing on and on.

They passed Mary's room. Through the small window in the door, Morrison could see her on the bed, restrained but sedated, her face turned toward the window. Even from here, he could see her eyes moving behind closed lids, dreaming of something.

"She'll be evaluated by our doctors tomorrow," Nurse Gladys said. "But tonight we'll let her rest. The journey from Port Augusta would have been very stressful for her."

They continued to a small office at the end of the hall. Nurse Gladys closed the door, and finally, blessedly, the radio noise faded to a muted hum.

She gestured to two chairs and sat behind a worn desk covered in files and papers.

"You want to know about Mary," she said. It wasn't a question.

"Everything," Morrison said. "From the beginning."

Nurse Gladys sighed, pulling a thick file from her drawer. "Mary Elizabeth Patterson. Born March 1953. Mother, Catherine Patterson, died in 1965 when Mary was twelve. Father..." she paused "Robert Patterson. Vietnam veteran. Currently listed as missing."

"Missing?" Peter leaned forward. "Not dead?"

"He disappeared four years ago. His car was found abandoned on a rural road outside of Perth. No body was ever recovered. Mary was the last person to see him alive."

Morrison felt a chill. "What happened?"

"Mary's story has been... inconsistent. Sometimes she says he drove off and never came back. Sometimes she says there was an accident. Sometimes she says she killed him." Nurse Gladys looked at them. "We don't know which version is true, if any of them are."

"But you suspect something," Morrison said.

Nurse Gladys chose her words carefully. "Robert Patterson was a Vietnam veteran. Came back changed, the way many of them did. His wife died of heart failure in 1965. After Catherine's death, Mary began making claims about her father. Claims we could never substantiate."

"What kind of claims?" Peter asked.

"She said he was hurting her. Abusing her sexually. Started saying this when she was around fourteen." Nurse Gladys's tone was measured, clinical. "A teacher noticed marks on her arms, reported it to authorities. Mary was removed from the home and brought here for evaluation."

"And what did the evaluation find?"

"Nothing conclusive. The marks could have been from restraints during one of her episodes, or self-inflicted, or from rough handling, we couldn't determine the source. Robert was investigated thoroughly. Social services, police, medical examiners. They found no evidence of abuse."

Morrison leaned forward. "No evidence at all?"

"No physical evidence of sexual abuse. No witnesses. No corroboration. Robert was a respected veteran, held down a steady job, maintained the house. Neighbours said he seemed like a devoted father." Nurse Gladys pulled out a document. "The investigating officer's report concluded that Mary's claims were likely the result of emerging psychiatric illness combined with unresolved grief over her mother's death."

"So she was lying?" Peter asked.

"Or she believed something that wasn't real. That's the problem with Mary, she's utterly convinced of her own narrative, but that narrative shifts depending on her mental state. Sometimes the abuse started when she was eight, sometimes ten, sometimes twelve. Sometimes it was nightly, sometimes weekly. The details never lined up."

"What happened after the investigation?"

"Mary was kept here for six months. Stabilised on medication, showed improvement. Robert visited regularly, seemed genuinely concerned about her recovery. The doctors felt she could safely return home with ongoing outpatient treatment." Nurse Gladys's expression was neutral. "That's how it went for years. She'd be home for a while, then have an episode, make more accusations, get admitted again. Then stabilise, go home, repeat."

"Why did you keep releasing her if she kept coming back?"

"Because we're a hospital, not a prison. If someone responds to treatment and has a safe home environment to return to, we release them. Robert always passed every evaluation. Model father. Patient, caring, willing to work with us."

Morrison felt uneasy. "But Mary kept insisting he was abusing her."

"Mary insisted many things that weren't real. She heard voices sometimes. Saw things. Had elaborate delusions about being followed, watched, threatened. The abuse narrative was consistent, yes, but so were some of her other delusions." Nurse Gladys pulled out another file. "This is from when she was sixteen. She was convinced that her dead mother was visiting her at night, telling her to run away. We found her trying to climb the fence at three in the morning, screaming that her mother was calling her. Was that real?"

The room fell silent.

"So you think the abuse was fabricated," Morrison said.

"I think Mary experienced trauma, her mother's death, her own mental illness, the upheaval of being institutionalised repeatedly. I think her mind created a narrative to explain her suffering. In her reality, her father was a monster. But in objective reality?" Nurse Gladys shrugged. "We found no proof."

"What happened four years ago?" Peter asked. "When Robert disappeared?"

"Mary was twenty. She'd been with us continuously for about three years at that point, the longest stretch she'd ever stayed. Robert had been approved for supervised visitation only, per court order during one of Mary's more severe episodes. Then one day, he showed up asking to take her on a day trip. Said he wanted to reconnect, help her recovery."

"And you let him?"

"The court restrictions had been lifted three months prior. Mary's doctors felt she was doing well enough for family outings. And Robert..." Gladys paused. "Robert seemed like he genuinely wanted to repair their relationship. He'd been coming every week, bringing her things, talking with her doctors. Everything pointed to this being therapeutic for her."

"What happened then?"

"They left in his car around noon. Mary seemed nervous but willing, she always was anxious around her father, but the doctors felt that was her mental illness making her suspicious, not genuine danger. They were supposed to be back by evening. But hours passed with no word. Then late that night, we got a call. Mary, incoherent, calling from a phone box on some rural road. All she could say was 'he's gone, he's gone, I made him stop.'"

Morrison leaned forward. "Where was Robert?"

"That's what everyone wanted to know. Police found his car about a hundred meters from where Mary was. Engine still running, driver's door open. Blood on the steering wheel. Blood on the seat. But no Robert. They searched the area, but nothing. No body. No trace of where he'd gone."

"And Mary?"

"Covered in blood. His blood. Hands scraped raw. Dissociating completely. She told them five different stories; he walked into the bush, he drove away, he never existed, she killed him and buried him, she killed him but he came back to life. None of it made sense." Nurse Gladys's voice was flat. "Eventually, they ruled it an unexplained disappearance. Mary was returned to us, and she's been here ever since."

"Do you think she killed him?" Morrison asked directly.

Nurse Gladys met his eyes. "I think Mary is capable of violence when she's in the grip of her delusions. If she believed Robert was attacking her—even if he wasn't—she might have defended herself. Whether that defence resulted in his death, or whether he simply abandoned her out there and disappeared on his own... we'll probably never know."

"You don't sound convinced she's dangerous," Peter observed.

"I'm convinced she's ill. There's a difference." Nurse Gladys closed the file. "Mary isn't evil. She's damaged, confused, trapped in a reality that doesn't match ours. When she killed those men on the highway, if she did kill them intentionally, it's because in her mind, she was killing her father. The monster she believes hurt her for years."

"Even though he might not have," Morrison said.

"Even though we have no proof he did," Gladys corrected. "That's the tragedy of Mary Patterson. She's been fighting a monster that may only exist in her own head. And now two innocent men are dead because of it."

"Until David Morrison," Peter said, changing subjects. "Tell us about David. Who was he? How did he know Mary?"

Nurse Gladys's expression tightened. "David started visiting us about a year ago. Said he had a friend here, Sarah Mitchell. Drug casualty, severe psychosis from LSD. He'd come every week to see her, spend an hour or so, then leave. But after a few months, I noticed he was spending time talking to Mary too."

"How did they meet?"

"Mary's room was next to Sarah's. David would pass by her door, see her sitting by the window. He started talking to her. Just casual conversation at first. Mary doesn't open up to people easily, especially men, but David..." Nurse Gladys paused. "David was persistent. Patient. Over months, Mary began to trust him."

"Was their relationship appropriate?"

Nurse Gladys looked away. "I thought so at the time. David seemed genuinely interested in her. He'd bring her books, sit with her for hours just talking. He never touched her inappropriately, never pushed boundaries. But..."

"But what?"

"But he became obsessed with her story. The abuse narrative. Mary would tell him about her father, and David would listen, and believe her." Nurse Gladys's tone held a note of disapproval. "He'd come to me, asking why we weren't protecting her, why we'd sent her back to Robert so many times. I tried to explain that Mary's claims had been investigated and found unsubstantiated, but David wouldn't accept that. He was convinced Mary was telling the truth and everyone had failed her."

"Maybe he was right," Morrison said quietly.

"Or maybe he enabled her delusions," Gladys countered. "Mary needs medication, therapy, reality-based treatment. Not someone validating beliefs that may not be real. David made her worse, in my opinion. She started regressing, having more episodes, becoming more paranoid. All because he kept reinforcing this narrative that she was a victim."

"When did the weekend release happen?"

"David approached me three months ago. Said he had family in Adelaide, an aunt who wanted to meet Mary, who had heard about her situation and wanted to help. He showed me paperwork, letters. It all looked legitimate. Mary was... well, she wasn't doing great, but she was stable enough. The doctors approved a supervised weekend visit."

"But there was no aunt," Peter said.

"No. I don't believe so now. David must have fabricated everything. And I..." Nurse Gladys's voice tightened. "I should have known. Should have checked more carefully. But David was so earnest, and Mary was so desperate to get out of here, and I thought maybe this could help her."

"When did you realise something was wrong?"

"Monday morning when she didn't come back. I tried calling David at an Adelaide address, but there was no answer. Tried the Perth address he'd listed, but it was a disconnected number. By Tuesday, I knew. He'd taken her. Whether to help her or hurt her, I didn't know, but he'd taken her."

The room fell silent except for the muted hum of the radio beyond the door.

"Do you think David loved her?" Morrison asked.

Nurse Gladys considered. "I think David loved the idea of rescuing her. He saw himself as her savior, the only one who believed her, the only one who cared. But real love? Real love would have meant getting her proper help, not enabling her illness."

"Did Mary love him?"

"Mary doesn't understand love normally. In her mind, every man is either her father or pretending to be safe until he can hurt her. I think sometimes she saw David clearly, as a kind man trying to help. But other times?" Gladys shook her head. "Other times I think she saw Robert. And maybe on that highway, under stress, she stopped seeing David at all and only saw the monster she believes hunted her for years."

"And defended herself," Peter finished.

"By killing the only person foolish enough to believe her stories and try to help." Nurse Gladys's voice was cold. "What a waste."

Morrison stood and walked to the window. Outside, the grounds of Greenplace stretched out, manicured lawns, a few trees, high fences in the distance. A bird landed on the window ledge, pecked at something, flew away.

"The knife," he said. "When we found Mary, she was carrying a knife. She said her father kept it under the seat 'for safety reasons.' Do you know anything about that?"

Nurse Gladys looked up. "Robert did carry a knife in his car. Large hunting knife. Mary became fixated on it after he disappeared. We found her with one once, stolen from the kitchen. She was just holding it, staring at it. We asked her why and she said, 'In case he comes back.'"

"In case her father comes back," Morrison said.

"Yes. In Mary's delusion, Robert never really died. He's still out there. Still hunting her. The knife is her protection against him."

"But she never used it," Peter observed. "She had it with her when we found her, but she never used it on James or David."

"Because in her mind, they didn't attack her the right way," Morrison realised. "The knife was for a specific scenario. If Robert came at her with a blade, she'd have a weapon. But James and David triggered different defence responses."

Peters blood went cold. The night he pulled her over, if she had thought his batten was a knife he may have...

He cleared his throat.

Nurse Gladys looked at him but carried on. "That's Mary's illness. Specific. Detailed. Every delusion tied to exact scenarios she's constructed about what Robert supposedly did to her."

Morrison turned back from the window. "One more question. Mary mentioned a name in her interview. Tommy. She said 'James and Tommy are dead.' Who is Tommy?"

Nurse Gladys's expression shifted, surprise, then understanding.

"Tommy," she said carefully, "was Mary's younger brother. Thomas Patterson. Died when Mary was fourteen. Fell from a second-story window. Mary was the only witness."

The room went very quiet.

"What exactly happened?" Morrison asked.

"Mary said Tommy was leaning out the window and lost his balance. But the investigating officer had doubts, the windowsill was too high for a ten-year-old to lean out far enough to fall unless he climbed on something. There was nothing to climb on. The room was clear."

"So someone pushed him," Peter said.

"The case was ruled an accidental death. But yes, someone probably pushed him. And Mary was the only other person in the room." Nurse Gladys met their eyes. "See what I mean? Mary's been dangerous for a very long time. Whether her father abused her or not, she's killed before. Her brother. Possibly her father. Now David and James. That's a pattern of violence that has nothing to do with self-defence."

Morrison felt sick. "Why wasn't this in our initial briefing?"

"Because it was ruled accidental. Juvenile records sealed. And because connecting it to Mary's current state would require admitting we released a potentially dangerous patient into the community." Nurse Gladys's voice was bitter. "The system protects itself, Detective. Always."

"What about the mother? Catherine? How did she die?"

"Heart failure. She was heavily medicated for depression and anxiety. The bottle of sleeping pills was empty beside her bed. Official cause was accidental overdose leading to cardiac arrest, but..." Gladys shrugged. "Mary was twelve. Home alone with her mother that weekend. Robert was away on a work trip."

The implications hung in the air.

"You think Mary killed her too," Morrison said.

"I think Mary has been killing people who she believes hurt her, or who get in her way, since she was a child. And she's learned to construct narratives that make it seem justified, or accidental, or like self-defence." Nurse Gladys stood. "That's the real Mary Patterson. Not a tragic victim. A deeply disturbed young woman who's been dangerous for over a decade, and who we failed to contain."

Morrison gathered his notes. "We'll need full access to Mary's files. Complete medical history. And we'll need to interview more staff, anyone who observed David and Mary's relationship."

"Of course. Whatever you need." Nurse Gladys moved toward the door. "Detective, what will happen to Mary now?"

"Psychiatric evaluation. She's not fit to stand trial. Most likely, she'll remain institutionalised. Here or somewhere more secure."

"So nothing changes," Nurse Gladys said. "After everything, she ends up right back where she started. Except now we know exactly how dangerous she is."

"She's not going anywhere," Morrison assured her. "She'll never have the chance to hurt anyone else."

As they left the office, the radio noise engulfed them again. Morrison glanced back toward Mary's room. The door was still closed, but he imagined her inside, hearing that sound, constructing new narratives about persecution and escape.

"The radio," he said to Nurse Gladys. "Why do you keep it on constantly?"

Nurse Gladys looked at him like he'd asked a stupid question. "Hospital policy. Music and voices help orient patients to reality, provide stimulation. Mary complains about it, but Mary complains about everything. It's part of her persecution complex; she thinks we're deliberately torturing her."

"Maybe you are," Peter muttered.

Nurse Gladys didn't respond.

Morrison thought about Mary in the car, probably frantically hitting the radio, begging David to turn it off. Mary at the cliff, hands over her ears. Mary in Port Augusta, panicking at the ambulance siren. A life lived in endless noise, real or imagined.

No wonder she watched the birds. In her delusion, they represented freedom. But there was no freedom for Mary Patterson. There never had been, and there never would be.

"We'll be back tomorrow," Morrison said. "To continue our investigation."

"I'll have everything ready for you," Nurse Gladys promised.

As they walked back through the corridors toward the exit, Morrison stopped at Mary's door one more time. Through the window, he could see her more clearly now. She was awake, sitting up despite the restraints, staring at the window. Her lips were moving, saying something over and over.

Morrison couldn't hear her through the door, but he could read her lips.

"Keep your eyes on the road. Keep your eyes on the road. Keep your eyes on the road."

Whatever those words meant to her, they were on an endless loop. Her mind's broken record, playing the same track over and over.

Peter touched his arm. "Come on. Let's get some rest. Tomorrow's going to be a long day."

They left Greenplace as the sun set over Perth, the building behind them lit up like a beacon against the darkening sky. Inside, the radio played on, and Mary Patterson watched the birds disappear into the night.

Believing, in her fractured reality, that her father was still out there somewhere.

When in truth, he might never have been the monster she claimed.

And that was the real tragedy, not what Robert Patterson had done to her, but what Mary's own mind had done to itself.

Chapter 16

Everything is fog. Thick, grey fog that rolls in and out like waves.

I'm moving. Or the world is moving around me. I can't tell which. Voices float above me, muffled and distant.

"...vitals are stable..."

"...should reach Perth by..."

"...poor thing, look at her..."

I try to open my eyes but my lids are so heavy. Like someone has placed weights on them. The world appears in brief flashes, white ceiling, moving lights, faces I don't recognise looking down at me.

Where am I?

Where's David?

I try to ask but my mouth won't work. My tongue is thick and clumsy. The words die before they reach my lips.

The fog rolls back in. I drift.

Time passes. Minutes? Hours? I don't know.

I surface again. This time I can feel more, the restraints on my wrists, the strap across my chest, the rocking motion of a vehicle. An ambulance. I'm in an ambulance.

Why am I in an ambulance?

A woman's face appears above me. Kind eyes. Nurse's uniform.

"It's okay, Mary. You're safe. We're taking you home."

Home. Greenplace. The word should make me feel something, but all I feel is the fog pulling me back down.

"...shouldn't have let her go..." a voice is saying. Another nurse, further away.

"...David was only helping..."

"...always the charming ones..."

David. They're talking about David.

I want to tell them David is good. David is kind. David is taking me to Adelaide where we can start fresh. But my mouth still won't work and the fog is so thick now.

I let it take me.

Sometime later, minutes? hours? days? I wake more fully. The restraints are still there but the fog has thinned slightly. I can see the ambulance interior more clearly. Two nurses sitting nearby, talking in low voices.

"...found two bodies..."

"...the American soldier..."

"...and David..."

"...ran him over with the car..."

No. That's not right. That's not what happened.

Or is it?

The memories are slippery. The cliff. The eyes watching me. Father's hands. The knife. The car. Blood.

So much blood.

I try to piece it together, but the fragments don't fit. Every time I think I have it, the fog rolls back in and scatters everything.

"...think she knew what she was doing..."

"...probably thought he was her father..."

"...poor David, trying to help and..."

Father. They said Father.

But Father is dead. I killed him. Didn't I?

Was that yesterday? Or years ago?

Time doesn't work right anymore.

The ambulance hits a bump, and I feel it through my whole body. The restraints dig into my wrists. I want to move, to stretch, to fly away like the birds. But I'm tied down. Trapped.

Always trapped.

The fog comes back, gentler this time. I don't fight it.

I dream of Tommy.

He's ten years old, catching fireflies in the backyard. His laugh is bright and clear like bells.

"Look, Mary! Look how many I caught!"

I'm fourteen again, watching him from the porch. "Don't hurt them, Tommy. They need to be free."

"I'll let them go," he promises. "I just want to look at them for a minute."

But then the memory shifts. We're inside now. Upstairs. The window is open.

"Don't lean out too far," I hear myself saying.

"I'm fine, Mary. I can see everything from here!"

And then.

No. I don't want to remember this part. I try to pull away from the memory but it has teeth. It holds on.

Tommy leaning too far. Tommy losing his balance. Tommy's eyes going wide with surprise and fear.

And my hand. Was my hand on his back? Pushing? Or reaching for him? Trying to catch him?

I can't remember. I can never remember.

"Tommy!" I scream, but no sound comes out because I'm sedated and restrained in an ambulance hundreds of kilometres from where it happened.

But Tommy still falls. Falls and falls and falls, forever falling in my memory, and I can never catch him.

"...she's dreaming..."

"...should we increase the sedation?..."

"...crying..."

Am I crying? I can't tell. Everything is wet and cold and the fog is so thick I can't see anything anymore.

Hands touch me. Gentle hands. A needle prick in my arm.

The fog becomes absolute.

When I wake again, everything is different.

I know this ceiling. These walls. This window.

I'm back.

Greenplace. My room. My bed.

The restraints are still on but they're different now, softer, attached to the bed frame instead of a gurney. The radio is playing somewhere. Not in my room, but close. In the hallway. That constant drone of voices and music and static that never stops never stops never stops.

I turn my head, slowly, because even that small movement makes the room spin, and look at the window.

It's daytime. The sun is streaming in. How long have I been asleep? Hours? Days?

There's a bird on the window ledge. A magpie. Black and white. It hops along the sill, pecks at something, looks in at me with one bright eye.

Free.

It's free.

The door opens. Nurse Gladys comes in, carrying a tray with pills and water.

"Mary," she says, her voice heavy with something I can't quite read. Sadness? Pity? Guilt? "You're awake. How are you feeling?"

How am I feeling?

I don't know how to answer that. I don't know how to explain that I feel like I'm scattered across hundreds of kilometres of empty highway. That pieces of me are still out there on the Nullarbor, at the cliff, in the car, in David's eyes as he...

"Where's David?" I ask. My voice is rough, unused.

Nurse Gladys's face crumples. "Oh, Mary. David is... David can't come see you anymore."

"Why not?"

"He's dead, love. He died on the highway. Don't you remember?"

Dead. The word doesn't mean anything. How can David be dead? He was just here. Or was that yesterday? Or a year ago?

"I don't remember," I whisper.

"That's okay. That's the sedation. It'll come back to you. Or maybe it won't. Maybe that would be better."

She sets the tray down on the bedside table and sits on the edge of my bed. Her weight makes the mattress dip.

"Mary, the police are here. At Greenplace. They want to talk to you again. They want to understand what happened. Can you tell me what you remember?"

What do I remember?

I remember the ocean. The cliff. The eyes watching me in the mirror. Father's hands. David's face changing into Father's face. Tommy falling. Always falling.

"I remember killing Father," I say.

Nurse Gladys goes very still. "Your father? Robert? Or David?"

"I don't know. Both? Are they different?"

She closes her eyes. "Yes, Mary. They're different people. David Morrison was your friend. He tried to help you. And he's dead now. Do you remember what happened to him?"

I try. I really try. But the memories won't line up. They keep sliding apart and rearranging themselves into different configurations.

"He grabbed me," I say slowly. "At the cliff. His hands on my shoulders. Just like Father used to. And I, I defended myself. I always defend myself."

"How did you defend yourself, Mary?"

"I hit him. With the car." The words come out flat, emotionless. Like I'm reading them from a script. "He was chasing me and I hit him with the car and he died."

"And the other man? James?"

James. The name triggers something. Fear. Panic. Eyes in the mirror.

"He was Father too," I whisper. "They're all Father. Every man who gets close, who tries to touch me, who looks at me with those eyes, they're all Father and I have to stop them before they hurt me again."

Nurse Gladys takes my hand. Her palm is warm. "Mary, your father is missing. He's been missing for four years. The men you killed, James and David, they weren't your father. They were just men who made the mistake of trying to help you."

"But Father always comes back," I insist. "I kill him but he always comes back. In new bodies. With new faces. But the same eyes. Always the same eyes."

"Oh, Mary," Nurse Gladys says, and there are tears on her face now. "What did he do to you? What did Robert do to make you like this?"

"Nothing," I say, because that's what I've always said. Because no one ever believed me anyway. "Father never hurt me. I made it all up. Everyone says so."

"But you believe he hurt you?"

"I don't know what I believe anymore. Maybe I'm the one who hurts people. Maybe I've always been the one. Mother. Tommy. Father. James. David." I look at her. "Did I kill them all?"

"I don't know," Nurse Gladys admits. "Maybe. Or maybe you're just very, very unlucky. Or maybe..." she stops.

"Maybe what?"

"Maybe you're sick in ways we don't understand yet. Ways we can't fix."

The magpie on the window flies away. I watch it go.

"I just wanted to be free," I whisper.

"I know," Nurse Gladys says. "I know you did."

She gives me the pills. I swallow them. They taste bitter but familiar. The fog starts to roll back in, gentler now, almost welcoming.

As I drift, I hear her talking to someone outside my door.

"...pattern of violence..."

"...present at five deaths..."

"...need to keep her sedated..."

"...may never be safe to release..."

The words float away. The magpie is gone. The birds are all gone.

There's only the radio now, playing its endless soundtrack of voices and static. And me, tied to a bed in a room with bars on the windows, watching the empty sky.

Waiting for Father to come back.

Because he always does.

Even when he's dead, he comes back.

And I'll be ready.

Chapter 17

Detective Morrison sat in Greenplace's administrative office the next morning, surrounded by a decade's worth of Mary Patterson's medical records. Peter was across from him, reading through incident reports and staff observations.

"Listen to this," Peter said. "Three years ago, Mary was found in another patient's room. The patient, elderly woman with dementia, had stopped breathing. Mary was sitting beside her bed, perfectly calm, said she was 'helping her sleep.' The woman died that night. Natural causes, they ruled it. But Mary was there."

Morrison looked up from the file he was reading. "How many incidents like that?"

"Six that are documented. All ruled natural causes or accidents. But Mary was present or nearby for all of them." Peter flipped pages. "Here's another, male orderly found unconscious at the bottom of a stairwell two years ago. Severe head trauma. He'd been checking on Mary's room. Claimed he slipped, but..."

"But Mary's door is nowhere near any stairs," Morrison finished, reading the floor plan.

"He had to go out of his way to get to that stairwell. Almost like he was running from something." Peter paused. "There's more. Staff reports show the orderly, Robert Chen, had been reprimanded twice for inappropriate behaviour toward Mary. Once caught touching her shoulder too long during a medication check. Another time found lingering outside her room after hours."

"So Mary could claim self-defence."

"If she pushed him. Which she denied. Said she was in her room the whole time, didn't see anything." Peter closed the file. "Chen survived but never came back to work. Refused to talk about what happened."

Morrison set down the file he'd been reading. "I've been going through Mary's early admissions. The first time she came here, she was fourteen. As Gladys said, Mary's school teacher reported suspicious bruises. When they examined her, they found some marks consistent with being grabbed or held down."

"So the abuse might be real?"

"Maybe. Or maybe the marks were from restraints during previous psychiatric episodes. Maybe self-inflicted. The examining doctor noted something interesting, Mary couldn't or wouldn't describe specific incidents. She'd say vague things like 'he comes at night' and 'he teaches me lessons' but when pressed for details, she'd change the subject or go silent."

"Trauma victims often can't talk about it," Peter offered.

"Or there's nothing specific to talk about because it's fabricated." Morrison pulled out a photograph of a young Mary, dead-eyed, staring at nothing. "This was taken after Tommy died. Look at her. No grief. No emotion. Just... blank."

"Maybe she's in shock."

"Or maybe she feels nothing because she's the one who killed him and feels no remorse." Morrison laid out more photographs. "I pulled the case file on Tommy's death. Ten-year-old boy, fell from a second-story window. Only witness was Mary. She claimed he was leaning out, lost his balance. But look at this." He pointed to a crime scene photo showing the open window. "The sill is at chest height for an adult. For a ten-year-old, it would be higher. He'd have to climb up on something to lean out far enough to fall."

"Was there anything to climb on?"

"No. The room was clear. No chair, no box, nothing. So either Tommy stood on his toes and leaned way out..."

"Or someone taller pushed him," Peter finished.

Morrison nodded grimly. "I called the original investigating officer. He's retired now, but he remembered the case. Said something always bothered him about it. The way Mary told the story, it was too perfect. Too rehearsed. Like she'd practiced it."

"And the mother? Catherine?"

"Heart failure, possibly from suffocation."

"Gladys didn't mention that.

"No she didn't. Catherine was found with a pillow over her face. Mary, age twelve, claimed she found her that way in the morning. But the medical examiner noted petechial haemorrhaging consistent with asphyxiation while the victim was unconscious or unable to fight back, which caused heart Failure. Catherine Patterson had been heavily medicated with sleeping pills. The bottle was empty beside her bed."

"Overdose and then suffocated?"

"Or suffocated by someone who knew she was too drugged to resist." Morrison pulled out another file. "And here's something interesting. Mary had been asking the household staff about her mother's sleeping pills. Wanted to know how many she took, whether they made her sleep deeply. This was two weeks before Catherine died."

Peter leaned back. "So Mary plans it. Asks about the pills. Waits until her mother is deeply asleep. Then suffocates her with a pillow. Makes it look like suicide or an accidental overdose."

"At twelve years old," Morrison added. "If that's what happened."

"Jesus. And two years later, Tommy."

"And four years ago, Robert disappears. Mary's the last person to see him alive. His car is found with blood but no body. And now James and David."

They sat in silence, the weight of it settling over them.

"Five deaths," Peter said quietly. "Catherine, Tommy, possibly Robert, definitely James and David. All with Mary present or involved. If she's been killing since she was twelve..."

"Then she's been doing it for over a decade and no one caught on because she's been institutionalized. The perfect cover. Everyone already thinks she's unstable, unreliable. Who would believe she's capable of serial murder?"

"But the abuse claims?"

"Could be real. Could be exaggerated. Could be completely fabricated." Morrison gathered the files. "That's the problem with Mary Patterson. We can't know what actually happened to her versus what she's constructed in her mind. And she might not know either."

"So what do you think? Victim or predator?"

Morrison was quiet for a moment. "I think she's learned that claiming abuse gets her sympathy. Gets people to make excuses for her behaviour. Gets staff members who question her labelled as insensitive or triggering. It's the perfect shield."

"That's pretty calculated for someone who's supposed to be delusional."

"Exactly."

A knock at the door. Nurse Gladys entered, looking exhausted.

"The doctor wants to see you. He's evaluated Mary this morning."

They followed her to another office where Dr. Kenneth Marsh, Greenplace's chief psychiatrist, waited. He was an older man, grey-haired, with tired eyes that had seen too much.

"Detectives," he greeted. "Please, sit. I understand you've been reviewing Mary's history."

"We have," Morrison said. "And we're seeing a disturbing pattern."

Dr. Marsh nodded slowly. "As am I. I've been Mary's primary psychiatrist for six years now. I've watched her closely, tried to understand her. And I'll be honest, I'm not entirely sure what I'm dealing with."

"Tell us what you see when you look at Mary."

"I see a profoundly disturbed young woman. She claims her father sexually abused her. She has some behaviours consistent with trauma. But..." Dr. Marsh hesitated. "There's no physical evidence. No corroboration. Her father was investigated when she was fourteen, social services, police, the works. They found nothing. No witnesses, no medical evidence of sexual abuse, nothing but Mary's claims. And her claims were... inconsistent."

"Inconsistent how?"

"The details changed depending on when you asked. Sometimes she'd say the abuse happened nightly. Other times weekly. Sometimes it started when she was six, other times when she was ten. The specifics never lined up." Dr. Marsh pulled out his notes. "What stayed consistent was the vagueness. She'd describe feelings, fear, pain, shame, but rarely concrete incidents. It's either severe dissociative amnesia from real trauma, or..."

"Or she's making it up as she goes," Morrison finished.

"I've considered both possibilities extensively. The truth is, I don't know. What I do know is that Mary has a remarkable ability to manipulate narrative. She believes what she's saying in the moment, I'm convinced of that, but the underlying truth? That's impossible to pin down."

"Do you think she was actually abused?"

Dr. Marsh was quiet for a long moment. "I think something happened in that house. Whether it was her father abusing her, or her mother's neglect, or witnessing something traumatic, or simply being a child with an emerging personality disorder in a dysfunctional family, I can't say. But I don't think any abuse was as extensive or as severe as Mary claims. I think she's built a narrative that explains her actions and absolves her of responsibility."

"Is she delusional?"

"Sometimes. She has genuine dissociative episodes where she loses time, where past and present blur. But other times..." Dr. Marsh met Morrison's eyes. "Other times I see perfect clarity. A calculation. An awareness of exactly what she's doing and how people will respond."

"Do you think she killed her mother and brother?"

"I think it's entirely possible. Mary was attached to Tommy, but she was also jealous of him. He was the normal one, the easy child. If she felt he was getting attention she deserved, or if he threatened to tell someone something she didn't want known." Dr. Marsh shrugged. "Children kill. It's rare, but it happens."

"And the mother?"

"Catherine Patterson was severely depressed. The sleeping pills, the withdrawal, all documented."

Morrison interrupted, "The Medical Examiners report listed heart failure as the cause of death. But it also suggested asphyxiation."

Suffocation, yes." Dr. Marsh pulled off his glasses. "Mary was asked to check on her mother that morning. She had access, opportunity, and possibly motive if Catherine was starting to suspect what Mary had done to Tommy."

"What about Robert? The father?"

"Here's where it gets interesting." Dr. Marsh pulled out another file. "Robert Patterson disappeared four years ago. Mary was with him the day, a supervised visit, the first in years. They were going to a local fair. He never came back. His car was found abandoned, blood everywhere inside, but no body."

"Mary's story?"

"She said he attacked her with a knife..."

"The one he kept under his car seat?" Peter asked.

"Yes. Although Mary was covered in blood, none of it her own. She had no cuts on her, just abrasions."

"You think Mary attacked Robert, with the knife that she knew would be under her seat?" Morrison asked.

"It's quite possible."

"If Mary knew the knife would be there and she willingly agreed to spend the day with Robert..." Peter paused. "Could this have been pre-meditated?"

"That's the million-dollar question, isn't it?" Morrison agreed.

Dr. Marsh stayed silent.

"Something bothers you about that?" asked Morrison.

"Yes," Dr. Marsh nodded. "Robert was supposed to be taking Mary for a day out at the local fair."

"He didn't?"

"No one saw them there, no witnesses. Mary herself has never mentioned the fair, not once."

"So where did they go?"

"No one knows. But the car and Mary were found fifty kilometres north of Perth, on a deserted coast road."

Peter looked at Morrison with even more questions. Questions he knew would never be answered. He leaned forward. "So she could have killed him out there?"

"Could have. But here's the thing, if she did, she hid the body well enough that it's never been found. That takes planning. Capability. Not the actions of someone in a dissociative fugue state."

Morrison felt cold. "You think she's a psychopath."

"I think she's something. Whether it's antisocial personality disorder, severe trauma response that's created a fractured sense of morality, or some combination, I don't know. What I do know is this: Mary Patterson is dangerous. The abuse narrative, real or fabricated, has become her shield. It makes people sympathetic. Makes them excuse her behaviour. Makes them blame everyone around her instead of looking at her actions."

"And David Morrison and James Coleman?"

Dr. Marsh's expression darkened. "Two more deaths. Mary claims she thought they were her father. Claims she was defending herself. And maybe in that moment, she genuinely believed it. Or maybe..." He paused. "Maybe she saw an opportunity. Two men, isolated, vulnerable. No witnesses. And she took it."

"That's premeditated."

"Is it? Or is it opportunistic violence from someone whose grip on reality is tenuous at best?" Dr. Marsh stood, moved to the window. "That's the impossible question with Mary. Where does the illness end and the intent begin? I've spent six years trying to answer that, and I'm no closer now than I was at the start."

"What happens to her now?" Peter asked.

"She stays here. Medicated. Constant supervision. Clearly the previous treatment didn't work, so we'll try something new."

"New? Like what?"

"Instead of dosing her up on medication, I'll reduce it. See if the real Mary will come out."

Morrison grunted. "What if this is the real Mary?"

"Then she'll never leave Greenplace again." Dr. Marsh turned back to them. "But I want you to understand something, this isn't justice. This is containment. Mary may live out her life in this facility, and we'll never truly know what happened in that house, or on that highway, or in any of the moments when someone around her died."

"Because we can't trust her word," Morrison said.

"Because we can't trust anyone's word when it comes to Mary Patterson. She's convinced some staff members she's a tragic victim. Others think she's manipulative. And the truth? It's probably somewhere in between, in a place we can't reach because Mary herself doesn't know where the truth is anymore."

Nurse Gladys, who'd been standing quietly by the door, spoke up. "She asks about her father sometimes. Wants to know if we've found him. If he's coming back."

"Does she seem afraid?" Morrison asked.

"Not afraid. More like..." Gladys struggled for words. "Like she's waiting for something. Like she knows something we don't."

The room fell silent.

Morrison gathered his notes. "We'll close the case on James Coleman and David Morrison. Deaths caused by Mary Patterson during a psychotic episode, diminished capacity, not fit to stand trial. She's already in custody for life. There's nothing more to prosecute."

"And the others? Catherine, Tommy, Robert?"

"Cold cases. Suspicious but unprovable. We can note the pattern, but without evidence..." Morrison stood. "Come on. Let's go talk to Mary one more time."

"You think she'll tell us anything?"

"No. But I need to see her. Try to understand what we're dealing with."

They walked through Greenplace's corridors, past patients and staff, the ever-present radio playing somewhere in the distance. When they reached Mary's room, Morrison looked through the window. She was sitting by her usual spot. Watching the sky. Waiting for birds.

"She looks so small," Peter said. "So fragile."

"That's what makes her effective," Morrison replied. "We see vulnerability and we want to protect. We don't see the danger until it's too late."

"Do you think the abuse was real? Any of it?"

Morrison watched Mary for a long moment. "I think something happened to that girl. But I also think she's killed multiple people and shows no real remorse. Both things can be true. And that's the tragedy, even if Robert Patterson did abuse her, it doesn't excuse what she became. It doesn't bring back the people she killed. It doesn't change the fact that she's dangerous."

"So what is she? Victim or monster?"

"Maybe she's both. Maybe that's the point, trauma doesn't excuse violence, but it can explain it. And explanation isn't the same as justification."

They stood there in silence, watching Mary watch the sky.

"She'll never leave here," Peter said quietly.

"No. She won't."

And perhaps, Morrison thought, that was the only real justice anyone would get. Not answers. Not closure. Just the knowledge that Mary Patterson would never hurt anyone else.

He turned away from the window. The case was closed. The files would be stored. And Mary would remain here, in this room, watching birds and waiting for a father who, if he was smart, would never come back. If he was alive at all. Morrison wasn't sure which scenario was worse.

Chapter 18

I sit in Dr. Marsh's office, hands folded in my lap like Nurse Gladys taught me. When you feel anxious, hold your own hands. It helps, sometimes.

"How are you sleeping?" Dr. Marsh asks.

"Better." My voice is steady. I've practiced this. "The nightmares are less frequent now."

"And the radio?"

I glance at the small transistor on his desk. It's silent right now, thank God. "I'm managing. Focusing on one voice at a time, like you said."

He makes a note. Always writing. Always documenting my progress.

"And your memories of the incident, have they become any clearer?"

The incident. That's what we call it. Not murder. Not killing. Just... the incident.

"I remember the road," I say carefully. "The ocean. Being scared. I remember thinking someone was trying to hurt me."

"Do you remember David Morrison?"

David. The name brings warmth and then cold. "Yes. He was kind. He was taking me to Adelaide." My throat tightens. "He was good."

"And do you remember what happened to him?"

My hands grip each other tighter. "I killed him. You told me I killed him. But when I try to remember, all I see is Father. His face. His eyes."

Dr. Marsh leans forward. This is the part where he corrects me. "Mary, we've talked about this. Your father disappeared four years ago. He wasn't on that highway. It was David Morrison and James Coleman. Two men who were trying to help you."

I've heard this before. Many times. The doctors, the nurses, even Detective Morrison, they all say the same thing. Father didn't hurt me. I made it all up. The abuse is in my head.

Maybe they're right. Maybe I am that crazy.

"I know," I say quietly. "I know Father wasn't really there. It was David and James."

Dr. Marsh nods, pleased. "That's real progress, Mary. How does it feel to accept that?"

"Confusing." I choose my words carefully. "I have these memories of Father hurting me. But everyone says they're not real. So I don't know what to believe."

"The mind can create very convincing false memories, especially when dealing with trauma. What matters is that you're learning to distinguish between what's real and what isn't."

I nod. I've stopped arguing about it. Every time I tried to explain, the late-night visits, the hands, the things he made me do, they'd exchange those looks. Poor delusional girl.

So now I keep those thoughts locked inside where no one can see them.

"I understand now that Father is gone," I say. "That he's been gone for four years. That what I thought I remembered... wasn't real."

Dr. Marsh smiles. "Excellent, Mary. Truly excellent progress."

I smile back. I've gotten good at this, saying what they want to hear.

I find my usual spot in the common room. The window seat where I can watch the birds.

There's a family of magpies in the tree outside. The mother brings food back every hour. I've been watching them for weeks now.

"You really love those birds," Nurse Gladys says, sitting beside me.

"They can fly away when things get bad."

"And you wish you could do that?"

"I used to." I watch a baby magpie hop along a branch. "Now I'm trying to understand that running away doesn't solve anything."

Gladys is quiet for a moment. Then: "Mary, can I ask you something?"

"Of course."

"Do you think your father hurt you? Really hurt you?"

I look at her. She's asking what she really thinks, not what the doctors say.

"Does it matter what I think? The doctors say there's no evidence. That I made it all up."

"I'm asking what you think."

I turn back to the window. "I think... I believe something terrible happened to me. Whether it actually did or not, I don't know anymore. Maybe I am just crazy."

"You're not crazy, Mary. You're ill. There's a difference."

I don't respond. What's the point? No one believes me. They never have.

"I won't talk about it anymore," I say finally. "I'll say what everyone wants to hear. That Father is gone. That he never hurt me. That it was all in my head."

"Mary..."

"It's fine, Gladys. Really." I watch the magpie take flight. "Maybe they're right anyway."

The courtyard garden is quiet this afternoon. Dr. Marsh suggested I spend time outside, "Fresh air and nature are good for the soul," he said.

I'm allowed thirty minutes three times a week. Supervised.

I sit on a bench near the flower beds, watching sparrows dart between the roses. The sun is warm on my face. For a moment, I can almost pretend I'm somewhere else. Somewhere normal.

A sharp crack splits the air.

I flinch, my whole body tensing. But it's just Mr. Fletcher, the groundskeeper. He's standing near the back fence with his shotgun, looking down at something in the grass.

"Got the bastard," he mutters, bending down to pick up a limp brown shape. A rabbit.

He notices me watching and gives a sheepish smile. "Don't worry, love. Just the rabbits. They're a pest, dig up all my flower beds." He walks closer, the dead rabbit dangling from his hand. "Wish I could shoot every creature that causes trouble around here. Make my job a lot easier."

He says it like a joke. Light-hearted. Grumbling the way old men do.

I manage a small smile. "I suppose they can be destructive."

"Too right they are." He nods toward the roses. "See those bare patches? All rabbit damage. Can't have nice things with pests around." He adjusts his shotgun. "Well, back to work. You enjoy the sunshine, eh?"

He walks off, whistling, the rabbit swinging in his grip.

I turn back to the sparrows. They've scattered from the gunshot but are slowly returning. Cautious. Alert.

Smart birds.

***

By my fourth month of being back here, I've learned to perform healing.

In group therapy, I say the right things. "I understand now that I was having a psychotic break. That David and James were real people trying to help me. That I killed them because my mind was broken."

The other patients nod sympathetically. Dr. Marsh looks pleased.

But late at night, alone in my room, I lie awake and remember. Father's breath on my neck. His weight. The things he whispered. Keep your eyes on the road, Mary. Don't look away.

Real or not real? I don't know anymore.

The doctors say it's not real. They're the experts. So I accept their truth and bury my own.

***

Five months in, Dr. Marsh reduces my medication again.

The clarity that comes is sharp. Painful.

I can think more clearly now. Can see my situation with brutal honesty. I killed two innocent men. Good men. David Morrison had dreams of working for the Space Agency. James Coleman was looking for peace after Vietnam.

And I took everything from them.

The guilt sits on my chest like a weight. Some days I can barely breathe under it.

"The guilt is good," Dr. Marsh tells me. "It means you're developing empathy."

But what do I do with it? How do I live with this?

"You accept it," he says. "And you work every day to be someone who wouldn't do that again."

I nod. Accept his wisdom.

But I know something he doesn't: I'm not getting better. I'm just getting better at hiding.

***

Six months after Port Augusta, something shifts.

I'm in session with Dr. Marsh, and he asks me to tell him about Father. "Not the abuse you think happened, we've established that was likely a coping mechanism. Tell me about the real Robert Patterson."

This is a test. I can feel it.

"He was a veteran," I say carefully. "Vietnam. He came back different. Broken. But he tried to be a good father."

"Go on."

"He taught me things. How to drive. How to be careful. He wanted to protect me." My voice is steady. "I think... I think maybe I blamed him for things that weren't his fault. Maybe I created this monster version of him because it was easier than accepting that sometimes bad things just happen."

Dr. Marsh writes quickly. "That's remarkable insight, Mary."

"I think he's dead now," I continue. "Wherever he went four years ago, he didn't come back. And I need to accept that. Accept that he's not coming back to hurt me, because he never hurt me in the first place."

"And how does it feel to say that?"

"Freeing." The lie comes easily now. "Like I can finally let go."

In truth, it feels like betrayal. Like I'm abandoning the little girl I was, the terrified child who needed someone to believe her.

But that child doesn't matter anymore. Only survival matters. Only saying what they want to hear.

Maybe one day, eventually, they'll start to believe my lies, and I'll get out of here. Run far away, so far no one will ever find me.

But for now. For now I keep telling their lies, because the refuse to hear the truth.

***

Seven months after everything fell apart, I stand at my window watching the sunset.

The magpies are settling in for the night. The babies are almost grown now. Soon they'll fly away and start their own lives.

I think about David. About the stars he showed me. About his kindness.

"I'm sorry," I whisper to the darkening sky. "I'm so sorry."

Behind me, the radio plays softly. I've been learning to tolerate it. To let the voices wash over me without panicking.

I've been learning to tolerate a lot of things.

The lies. The disbelief. The constant performance of sanity.

But at least I'm getting better at it. At pretending. At saying what they want to hear.

At accepting that Father is dead and gone.

Even though some part of me, the part I never speak about, still feels him watching. Still feels him waiting.

The sun disappears below the horizon. The birds settle into silence.

And I turn away from the window, ready to face another day of careful lies and managed truth.

Ready to be the Mary they want me to be.

Even if it means abandoning the Mary I actually am.

Chapter 19

Nine months after Port Augusta.

I stand in front of the mirror in my room, smoothing down the plain beige dress they've given me. It's shapeless. Institutional. Nothing like...

"Can I wear my polka dot dress instead?" I ask Gladys. "The red one with the white dots? For the hearing?"

Gladys's expression shifts. Sad. Pitying. "Mary, love, that dress was thrown out when you arrived. It was covered in blood. We couldn't get it out."

"Oh." I keep my face neutral. "Okay."

But inside, a small voice whispers: It was his favourite.

I push the thought away and reach for the pale blue cardigan. Button it neatly. One button at a time.

"You look lovely, Mary," Gladys says from the doorway. "Ready for the hearing?"

The hearing. The psychiatric review board will decide if I'm fit to stand trial for what I did to David and James. Dr. Marsh says I won't be. Says I'll stay here at Greenplace. Locked, safe, but not restrained. Protected from the world and the world protected from me.

"As ready as I'll ever be," I say.

Gladys helps me straighten my collar. My hair is clean and brushed. I look like someone who's getting better. Someone who's healing.

I've gotten very good at looking like things I'm not.

***

The hearing room is smaller than I expected. A long table with three people behind it, two men and a woman, all looking tired and official. Dr. Marsh sits to one side. A court-appointed psychiatrist I don't know sits on the other. And I'm in the middle, hands folded in my lap.

"Miss Patterson," the woman begins. She has kind eyes but a stern mouth. "We're here to determine your fitness to stand trial for the deaths of David Morrison and James Coleman. Do you understand why you're here?"

"Yes, ma'am."

"Can you tell us, in your own words, what you remember about the incident?"

I take a breath. I've practiced this. "I remember being on the highway with David. He'd picked me up from Greenplace. He was taking me to Adelaide." My voice is steady. Calm. "We picked up James somewhere along the way. A hitchhiker. And then..."

I pause. Let my voice tremble just slightly. "And then I started to get confused. I thought, I thought they were someone else. Someone who was going to hurt me. But they weren't. They were just good people trying to help. And I killed them because I couldn't tell the difference between past and present."

One of the men leans forward. "Who did you think they were?"

"My father." The lie comes easily now. "I thought my father had come back. But he's dead. He's been gone for four years. It was just my broken mind making me see things that weren't there."

Dr. Marsh nods approvingly from his seat.

"And do you understand that what you did was wrong?" the woman asks.

"Yes." I meet her eyes. "I killed two innocent men. Nothing can change that. Nothing can bring them back. I have to live with that every day."

"Dr. Marsh," the woman says, turning to him. "Your assessment?"

Dr. Marsh stands. "Mary Patterson suffers from severe PTSD with dissociative features. At the time of the incident, she was experiencing a complete break from reality. She genuinely could not distinguish between past trauma and present circumstances. She believed she was defending herself against an active threat when, in fact, no threat existed."

"And now?"

"Now, with the right medication and intensive therapy, Mary has made remarkable progress. She understands what happened. She experiences genuine remorse. However," He pauses. "She remains fragile. Institutionalisation is essential, both for her safety and for public safety. She needs a controlled environment with ongoing psychiatric care."

"So you're not recommending trial?"

"Absolutely not. Mary Patterson is not fit to stand trial. She was not in her right mind during the incident and prosecuting her would serve no purpose. She needs treatment, not punishment."

The board members confer quietly among themselves. I sit very still. Very small. Exactly as they expect me to be.

Finally, the woman speaks. "Mary Patterson, this board finds you not fit to stand trial due to diminished capacity. You will remain at Greenplace Psychiatric Facility under indefinite civil commitment. You will continue treatment and be subject to annual reviews. Do you understand?"

"Yes, ma'am. Thank you."

Relief washes through the room. Dr. Marsh smiles. Gladys squeezes my shoulder.

I've won. I get to stay here. Safe. Protected.

Trapped.

***

One year after Port Augusta.

The seasons have changed. Winter has come and gone. Spring arrived with new birds and new flowers in the courtyard garden that patients are sometimes allowed to visit.

I'm allowed any time, still supervised, but the air is good for me. It's freeing.

I sit on a bench, watching sparrows fight over breadcrumbs someone scattered on the path. The sun is warm on my face. If I close my eyes, I can almost pretend I'm somewhere else. Somewhere free.

"You're doing so well," Dr. Marsh said in our session this morning. "Your progress has exceeded all expectations. A year ago, you could barely speak coherently. Now look at you, engaged, aware, emotionally regulated. It's remarkable."

I thanked him. Smiled. Said all the right things.

But the truth is, I feel hollowed out. Like I've carved away pieces of myself to fit into the shape they want. The Mary who remembers Father's hands, I've locked her away in some deep, dark place where no one can hear her screaming.

Yet she silently screams every night.

The Mary who sits on this bench in the sunshine? She's someone else entirely. Someone manageable. Someone safe.

Someone fake.

"Mary?"

I open my eyes. Angela, my friend from group therapy, sits down beside me. She's been here for three years. Domestic violence PTSD. She understands what it's like to see threats everywhere.

"Hey," I say.

"You seem sad today."

"Just thinking."

"About what happened?"

"About everything." I watch the sparrows. "Do you ever feel like you're just... pretending to be better? Like you're performing recovery for everyone else?"

Angela is quiet for a moment. "Every single day."

"Does it get easier? The pretending?"

"Yes and no." She picks at a thread on her sleeve. "It gets easier to do. But it gets harder to remember who you actually are underneath it all."

"What if there's nothing underneath? What if the pretending is all there is?"

"Then I guess we're all just empty shells walking around, hoping no one notices." She smiles sadly. "But I don't think that's true. I think the real us is still in there. Just buried. Waiting."

"Waiting for what?"

"I don't know. Maybe for someone to finally believe us."

I look at her. "No one's going to believe us, Angela."

"I know." She stands up. "But maybe someday we'll believe ourselves again. That's something, at least."

She walks away, leaving me with the sparrows and the sunshine and the hollow feeling in my chest.

***

Fourteen months after Port Augusta.

Dr. Marsh reduces my medication again. I'm on the lowest dose I've been on in a decade. My mind is sharp. Clear. Sometimes too clear.

I remember things now that I'd rather forget. Not just Father, though those memories are there, vivid and terrible in the dark, but also the good things. Mother singing. Tommy laughing. The house by the river before everything went wrong.

I remember being a child who believed in good things. Who thought the world was safe.

I don't know when I stopped believing that. Maybe when Father first came to my room. Maybe when Mother took those pills. Maybe when Tommy's eyes met mine in the window glass.

Or maybe I never really believed it at all.

"Tell me about your future," Dr. Marsh says during our session. "What do you see for yourself?"

My future. What a strange concept.

"I see... staying here. Getting better. Maybe helping other patients someday, if I'm allowed. Being useful."

"That's very grounded. Very realistic." He makes a note. "But what about dreams? What would you want if you could have anything?"

I think about David's stars. About Adelaide. About the feeling of my arm out the car window, pretending to fly.

"I want to get away, far away. I'd want to be free," I say quietly. "Not just physically. But free from... from the past. From the memories. From always feeling like I'm waiting for something terrible to happen."

"That's a beautiful goal, Mary. And I think it's achievable. Not the forgetting, trauma doesn't work that way. But the freedom from fear? That's possible. With time and work, you can get there."

I nod. Let him believe I believe him.

But I know the truth. The fear is part of me now. It's woven into every thought, every breath. I'll never be free of it.

I'll never be free of him.

***

Fifteen months after Port Augusta.

Nurse Gladys finds me crying in my room. Not the dramatic, hysterical crying from before. Just quiet tears, rolling down my cheeks as I sit by the window.

"What's wrong, love?"

"I miss him," I whisper. "I miss David. I know I shouldn't, I know I killed him, but I miss him so much it hurts."

Gladys sits beside me. "Tell me about him. What do you miss?"

"His kindness. The way he looked at me like I was... like I was worth something. Like I mattered." The tears come faster now. "He was taking me to Adelaide. He had dreams. And I destroyed all of that because I'm so broken I can't tell the difference between someone trying to help me and someone trying to hurt me."

"You were sick, Mary. You didn't choose to be sick."

"But I still did it. And he's still dead. And his family still lost him. And it's still my fault."

Gladys doesn't argue. She just sits with me while I cry. Sometimes that's all there is, sitting with the pain because there's no way to fix it.

"Do you think I'll ever forgive myself?" I ask when the tears finally stop.

"I don't know. But I think you can learn to live with it. To carry it without letting it destroy you."

"And if I can't?"

"Then we keep trying. Day by day. That's all any of us can do."

***

Sixteen months after Port Augusta.

The anniversary of Mother's death passes. I mark it privately, alone in my room. Seventeen years since I found her with the pillow over her face. Seventeen years of wondering if I could have saved her.

Seventeen years of knowing, deep down, that I didn't want to.

I don't tell Dr. Marsh this. Don't tell anyone. Some truths are too dark to speak aloud.

But I think about her sometimes. About how she'd take those sleeping pills and disappear into unconsciousness while Father...

No. Stop. He's dead. He's gone. The abuse wasn't real.

That's what they tell me. That's what I'm supposed to believe.

So I push the memories away and focus on being good. Being cooperative. Being the patient they want me to be.

***

Seventeen months after Port Augusta.

Dr. Marsh calls me into his office with news.

"Mary, I wanted to let you know that we're going to be easing some restrictions. You've earned it with your progress."

"What kind of restrictions?"

"You'll have more freedom to move around the facility unsupervised. Access to the library. Outdoor time without constant monitoring. We trust you now."

Trust. What a strange word.

"Thank you," I say. "I won't let you down."

"I know you won't." He smiles. "You've come so far, Mary. I'm very proud of you."

Pride. Another strange word.

I leave his office and walk through the corridors of Greenplace. My prison. My home. The walls that keep me safe and trapped in equal measure.

More freedom, they say. But it's still not real freedom. Still just a longer leash.

But I smile and nod and say thank you because that's what they expect.

And because somewhere deep inside, I'm still that little girl who learned that survival means being small and quiet and saying what they want to hear.

Even if it's killing me slowly from the inside out.

***

Eighteen months after Port Augusta. Late September.

It's visiting day at Greenplace. I usually stay in my room during visiting hours, I don't have anyone to see me, but today Dr. Marsh suggested I spend time in the common room. "Exposure to normal family interactions," he said. "It's good for you to see healthy relationships."

So I sit by my window, watching the magpies, while other patients greet their families. Mothers. Fathers. Sisters. Brothers. Children. People who haven't given up on them.

I decide to step outside for some air. The courtyard is busy with visitors strolling through the gardens.

Mr. Fletcher walks past me, shotgun cracked open over his arm. He gives me a nod and a small smile.

"More rabbits?" I ask.

"Maybe." He glances toward the trees at the edge of the property. There's a rustling in the branches, something moving.

He stops. Cocks his gun closed with a sharp click.

"Excuse me, love," he says, and walks off toward the sound, gun ready.

I watch him disappear into the shadows of the trees, then turn back toward the building. The common room feels safer somehow.

Angela's mother is here, a small woman with grey hair who holds her daughter's hands and speaks softly. I watch them and feel something hollow open up inside me.

A couple walks past, older, maybe in their fifties. The woman has kind eyes and the man walks with a slight limp. They're here to see their daughter, I think. I've seen the girl, Rachel, in group therapy sometimes.

The man glances at me as they pass. Then stops. Looks again.

"Excuse me," he says, turning back. "Are you... Mary Patterson?"

My chest tightens. "Yes."

"I thought so. I recognised you from the newspapers." He pauses. "I'm sorry, I don't mean to intrude. It's just, I used to know your parents. Robert and Catherine Patterson, right? From over by the Swan River?"

Catherine. Mother. Someone who remembers her.

"Yes," I say quietly. "Did you know them well?"

"We lived in the neighbourhood for a few years. Our daughter played with you once or twice, though you probably don't remember. You were very young. But I remember your mother, lovely woman. She used to sing in the church choir."

Something warm spreads through my chest. "She did. She had a beautiful voice."

"She did indeed." He smiles. "And you, I remember you playing in the garden. Always watching the birds, even back then. Your mother used to say you'd be a ornithologist someday."

I feel tears prick my eyes. Someone remembers. Someone saw me as a child, before everything went wrong.

"Thank you," I whisper. "Thank you for remembering her."

"Of course." He glances at his wife, who's waiting patiently. "Well, we should let you get back to your birds. Robert always says you have a gift with them."

Robert. Father's name. Present tense.

But before I can process it, he's already moving on. "Your mother would be so proud of how far you've come, Mary. She always worried about you, but she loved you dearly."

loved you dearly."

I smile, my throat tight. "Thank you for remembering her." I say again.

He smiles warmly and walks away with his wife, leaving me by the window.

I sit back down, a warm feeling still glowing in my chest. Someone remembered Mother. Someone saw her as more than just a tragedy in the newspapers. Someone knew her voice, her kindness, her love.

I spend the rest of visiting hours thinking about Mother in the church choir. About playing in the garden as a child. About being small and safe and loved.

That night, lying in bed, the man's words come back to me for just a moment.

Robert always says. Present tense.

I turn over, pull the blanket higher. It was nothing. Just an old man's way of speaking. I was too focused on hearing about Mother to notice much else anyway.

Outside my window, the night is dark and still.

I close my eyes and let sleep take me.

Chapter 20

October 1979.

Dr. Marsh gathers us in the common room. All the patients who are well enough to understand. There must be twenty of us, sitting in rows of chairs, waiting.

"I have an announcement," he says. His voice is steady but I can see the tension in his shoulders. "Greenplace will be closing at the end of the year. The government has decided to redirect funding toward community-based care programs."

Silence. Then murmurs. Angela grabs my hand.

"What happens to us?" someone asks.

"You'll be transferred to other facilities or, for those who are ready, transitioned into supervised community housing. We'll be evaluating each patient individually over the next few months to determine the best placement."

My chest tightens.

Closing.

Greenplace is closing. This place has been my home for twelve years. On and off, yes, but always here. Always the same walls, the same windows, the same routine. Safe. Predictable.

And now it's ending.

"Change is difficult," Dr. Marsh continues. "But it's also an opportunity. Some of you have made remarkable progress. This could be your chance at a more normal life."

Did Dr. Marsh's eyes just linger on me? I brush the thought aside.

A more normal life. What does that even mean for someone like me? I'm twenty-six years old and I've spent nearly half my life behind these walls.

After the meeting, I sit by my window. The birds are still there. Honeyeaters flitting between branches, wattlebirds calling their harsh songs. They don't know that everything is about to change. They'll just keep living their simple lives, keep flying.

Lucky them.

"How are you feeling about the news?" Dr. Marsh asks during our next session.

"Scared," I admit. "This is the only place I feel safe."

"Safe from what, Mary?" I pause. Careful. "Safe from myself. From making mistakes. From hurting people."

"You've made tremendous progress. You haven't had a dissociative episode in over a year. Your medication is stable. You're ready for the next step."

"But what if I'm not? What if the structure here is the only thing keeping me... okay?"

Dr. Marsh leans forward. "Mary, you've done the work. You've learned coping mechanisms. You understand your triggers. Yes, you'll always need support, but you don't need to be locked away forever. That's not living."

"But what if..." I can't finish. What if I see Father again? What if I hurt someone? What if, what if, what if?

"We'll find the right placement for you," he says gently. "Somewhere safe. Somewhere you can continue to heal."

I nod. Say the right things. But inside, I'm terrified.

Change is dangerous. Change means unpredictability. And unpredictability means losing control.

***

November 1979.

The evaluations begin. Each patient is assessed, interviewed, categorized.

Some will go to other psychiatric facilities, the ones who need constant care, who can't function outside institutional walls.

Some will go to halfway houses, supervised group homes where they'll learn to reintegrate slowly. And a lucky few will go home. Back to families who still want them. Back to lives they left behind.

I don't know which category I'll fall into. I don't have family. I can't live alone. But I'm too functional for constant supervision.

I'm in between. Always in between.

"We're considering a few options for you," Dr. Marsh tells me. "There's a group home in Fremantle that specializes in trauma cases. Or there's a supervised apartment program where you'd have weekly check-ins."

Both sound terrifying. Too much freedom. Too much trust.

"Can't I just... transfer to another facility? Like Greenplace but somewhere else?"

"Mary, that's not the direction mental health care is going. The goal is independence, not permanent institutionalisation. You're twenty-six years old. You deserve a chance at a real life."

A real life. What does that look like for someone who's killed four people? Maybe five, if you count Father's disappearance.

But I don't say this. I just nod.

***

December 1979.

The facility is winding down. Staff are leaving for new positions. Patients are being transferred in waves. The walls feel emptier each day.

Angela left last week. Went to a halfway house in Perth. She hugged me goodbye and whispered, "We survived. Remember that. We survived."

But did we? Or are we just pretending?

I spend most of my time by the window. The tree outside is quiet today. Even the birds seem to sense something ending.

I'm sitting in my chair when I hear footsteps approaching. My body tenses automatically.

"Mary?"

Gladys stands in my doorway. She's one of the few staff members staying until the very end. Making sure everyone is settled before she moves on.

"They've made a decision about your placement," she says.

My heart pounds. "Where?"

"Actually..." She smiles. Genuine warmth in her eyes. "We have found something perfect. Lives in the country, away from anyone. Someone who's just right to look after your needs. A private arrangement. Someone with experience, someone who understands your history."

"Who?"

"Let me bring them in. They're here now, actually. Came all this way to meet you."

My hands start to shake. "Gladys, I don't, I'm not ready to meet anyone. Can we do this another day?"

"Mary, it's going to be fine. Trust me. This person really cares about you."

She disappears before I can protest.

I stand up. My legs are shaking. I move to the bed, curl up on my side facing the window. Make myself small. One, two, three. One, two, three.

Footsteps in the corridor. Getting closer.

I should run. I should hide. But where would I go? Greenplace is closing. There's nowhere to run to anymore.

The footsteps stop outside my door.

A smell reaches me. Old Spice cologne and cigarette smoke and something else. Something familiar. Something that makes every muscle in my body lock up.

No.

No, no, no, no, no.

Gladys appears in the doorway. Smiling. Pleased with herself.

"Mary, this is Robert Patterson. Your father. He's been living in the country for the past few years, but when he heard Greenplace was closing, he came forward. He wants to take you home, sweetheart. Isn't that wonderful?"

Behind her, a man steps into view.

Tall. Greying hair. Eyes that are the same colour as mine. Eyes that I've seen in every nightmare, every flashback, every moment of terror for the past nineteen years.

Eyes that are real.

He's real.

He was always real.

Father smiles. That smile. The one that looks kind to everyone else but holds everything terrible underneath.

"Hello, Mary," he says. His voice is exactly as I remember. Soft. Gentle. Wrong. "There's my special little girl. Daddy's come to collect you. Bring you home."

The room tilts. My vision tunnels.

I can't breathe. Can't think. Can't speak.

I look at Gladys. Really look at her. My eyes pleading. Begging. Screaming silently: Help me. Please. You have to help me. He's going to hurt me. Please believe me. Please.

But Gladys just smiles wider. Misreads everything in my expression.

"I know, love," she says softly. "It's overwhelming. But it's happy tears, isn't it? Your father's come back for you."

And in that moment, I understand with perfect, horrible clarity: no one is going to help me.

No one is going to save me.

No one ever believed me, and no one ever will.

Father takes a step into the room. Just one step.

I curl tighter into myself. Make myself smaller. So small. As small as I can be.

When you're small, you're harder to see. And when you can't be seen, bad things can't find you.

But he's already found me.

He's always been there. Always watching. Always waiting.

"I know this is overwhelming, sweetheart," Father says, still smiling. "But everything's going to be fine now. You're coming home. Just like old times."

Just like old times.

"It's okay to cry, Mary," Father says softly, moving closer. "I know you've been through a lot. But Daddy's here now. Everything's going to be just fine."

His hand reaches out.

Touches my shoulder.

And I close my eyes.

Make myself smaller.

Count.

One, two, three.

One, two, three.

One, two, three.

Father's grip tightens. Just slightly. Just enough.

"Let's go home, Mary," he whispers. "It's time."

And somewhere deep inside, the little girl who tried so desperately to tell everyone the truth, the girl no one believed, finally stops screaming.

Because what's the point?

He was always real.

The monster was always real.

My eyes drift to the window one last time.

Outside, high against the blue sky, a lone eagle circles. Up and up and up. Flying away. Flying toward freedom.

I watch it, this last beautiful thing. This last piece of hope.

Then, a sound. Sharp. Distant. Like a car backfiring somewhere on the road below.

The eagle jerks in mid-flight.

Falls.

Tumbles from the sky in a spiral of feathers and failing wings.

Down.

Down.

Down.

Until I can't see it anymore.

A single tear rolls down my cheek.

I don't wipe it away.

Father's hand is warm on my shoulder.

And I know, with complete and terrible certainty, that I will never fly away.

Not now.

Not ever.